TO THE ABSAROKA

(BUCKSKIN CHRONICLES BOOK 3)

B.N. RUNDELL

WOLFPACK
PUBLISHING
— EST 2013 —

To The Absaroka
(Buckskin Chronicles Book 3)
B.N. Rundell

Paperback Edition
Copyright © 2018 by B.N. Rundell

Wolfpack Publishing
6032 Wheat Penny Avenue
Las Vegas, NV 89122

ISBN: 978-1-62918-558-3

This is dedicated to the love of my life, without her this and any other work ever accomplished by me would not have been possible. Her support, inspiration, and encouragement gives meaning to each and every day and purpose to my life. My wife, Dawn, has faithfully been by my side for over a half-century and she's planning on that much more. So, thank you, my beloved. And to my children and grandchildren who have repeatedly expressed their pride in this old man and have continually been a source of pride for me and mine.

TO THE ABSAROKA

Awakened early by a lazy but insistent owl that couldn't find his mate by echoing his hooting throughout the small pine framed valley, Jeremiah stretched to his full height and looked down on the still form of his wife, Laughing Waters. With a smile on her still sleeping face, he wondered what she was dreaming to put such a look of contentment on what he thought was the most beautiful face he had ever seen.

Even as he stepped to the coals of the previous night's fire to stir it to flame, he marveled at his good fortune to have this woman as his life mate. He never imagined the depth of love he felt for her and his amazement that she returned every bit of that affection. The growing light from the smokeless fire shared its glow with the towering ponderosa pine that framed the familiar clearing.

This was the place that harbored the grave of his old friend and mentor, Ezekiel, also known as Buffalo Thunder, the man that rescued Jeremiah as a youth and reared him to manhood. It was from Ezekiel that he gained his knowledge of the mountains and more than that, every aspect of character and integrity that he possessed, he'd learned from the big escaped slave.

It was here in this clearing and in the shadow of the mountain that the hard lessons were learned. Now, looking toward the towering granite and at the base of the mountain, he remembered the cabin that was their home when they were away from the Arapaho village. It was just over yonder down that trail to the creek where they labored together extracting the gold dust that was to enable Jeremiah to fulfill the promise made to Ezekiel, the promise to free his family from the bondage of slavery. A promise fulfilled.

As his gaze returned to the base of the mountain, he admired his handiwork of the new cabin rising from the ashes of the old, and hoped he would be able to instill in his nephew the same values and character. Remembering the death-bed promise he made to his sister to raise Caleb to be a man, he felt the responsibility heavy on his shoulders. He was continually surprised at the boy and his many talents, especially when it came to his mimicry of every animal of the woods. To be able to duplicate the call of every bird and animal was amazing to Jeremiah. And the boy had grown so much in the past two years; he was just over shoulder height to Jeremiah and was filling out like a man at only twelve years old.

Shaking his head that seemed to be so full of reflections and wonder this early in the morning, he grabbed the coffee pot and headed to the creek for fresh water. Returning to the fire, he placed the pot on the flat rock near the flame and turned to get a handful of coffee beans from the parfleche to start grinding them on the stone. The aroma from the beans made his stomach grumble in protest at the early morning and caused Jeremiah to hurry the grinding and drop the coffee into the warming water. Two soft hands touched his shoulders and began to massage the corded muscles beside his neck.

"Mmmm, woman, you can keep that up till noon, if'n ya want. I won't mind at all," said the buckskin clad mountain man as he turned to see the smiling eyes of his wife. Standing to take her in his arms, he kissed her like he had just returned from a long absence. She responded with a tip-toe stretch and both arms around his neck to pull his face down to hers. The growing swell of her belly fit comfortably against his and he was reminded of the new life she bore for them. It had become his habit to be clean-shaven even though most white men of the mountains preferred whiskers, Waters liked to see his face and although Jeremiah had sported a full beard on the trip to and from the East, he was more comfortable being clean-shaven.

Echoing the sentiment of her husband, Waters said, "Mmmm, husband, you can keep that up till noon, if you want, I won't mind at all," as she smiled mischievously up at her man. Then pushing herself away, she made busy with preparations for the morning meal. "You should take Talks to the Wind down to the creek and scrub him till you find him. He smells!" Talks to the Wind was the tribal name for Caleb because of his ability to talk with the animals. When he first came to the village, Black Kettle, the father of Waters, called him Bear Cub, but as they learned of his gift of sounds, he earned a man's name and Black Kettle gave him the name Talks to the Wind. He had been a big help as they labored on the new cabin, but taking a bath wasn't his favorite activity and often had to be coerced. "When you are done, the meal will be waiting."

The man and his shadow followed the trail to the creek and the shallow pool below the rocker box. Both stripped off their buckskins and waded into the water to begin the necessary scrubbing with soap root and sand. Responding to the call from Laughing Waters, they quickly climbed out and after wiping off, hurriedly put the buckskins back on and raced each other to the camp-fire. The hungry men readily devoured the fresh fried deer liver, wild onions, and biscuits and gravy without wasting time on breakfast conversation. Setting his tin plate aside, Jeremiah stretched out and patted his belly, let out a big belch, and said, "Woman, I do believe that every meal just gets better 'n better. You keep feedin' us like this, we'll both be too fat ta' get any work done. Ain't that right, squirt?" he asked Caleb.

"Speak for yourself. You keep sayin' I'm a growin' boy and I need all the vittles I can get!"

"But yore gonna have ta' keep growin' just ta' have room fer all ya' been eatin'," observed his Uncle.

With a slight smile and a motion of her hand, Laughing Waters instructed Caleb to take the plates and other utensils to the creek to wash. Turning to Jeremiah, she said, "While you work on the cabin, I will make meat and gather other things," referring to the many berries and other wild plants that supplemented their meals. Her ability with the bow made her an excellent hunter and enabled Jeremiah to spend more time working on the cabin to prepare their home for the coming winter.

The first two years of their life together, they lived with Waters' village and family, but they both wanted more time alone and the opportunity to build their lives together. The work on the cabin was difficult but rewarding and the family enjoyed seeing their dream become reality. The walls were up, the ridge pole set and today's work was to place the rafters and finish the roof. Jeremiah had taught Caleb how to split the cedar to make the shake roof. During his travels to and from Kentucky, Jeremiah had observed and studied the construction of many cabins and logged the knowledge away for this day. Caleb had accumulated a considerable stack of shakes, but more would be needed.

After their mid-day break, Jeremiah said to Caleb, "We'll go see about gettin' some more cedar. I think there's a couple more over past that other draw down below, it's getting' kinda hard to find any that have any straight trunk to 'em ta' get enough shakes outta 'em, but I think those two'll do the job."

"Do ya' think they'll be dry enough?" asked the boy.

"Well, what with the drought an all this summer, a lot o' them trees ain't been gettin' 'nuff water to stay green, and they're startin' to die off. That spot over yonder ain't seen water in a couple years, so I think they'll be all right," concluded Jeremiah. They were fortunate to have the tools that Jeremiah traded for on their return trip to the Wind River range. The stop at the Fontenelle trading post yielded the tools, a saw, axes, and a hoe that were necessary for the construction of the home. It was unusual for a trader to have the tools, but he had received them in trade from a destitute carpenter desperate to return to his home in the East.

This summer had been unusually hot and dry. The second year of drought was taking its toll on both plants and animals with the animals suffering the most. Many of the bigger game had already sought higher country or more distant lands further North in their search for greener graze and ample water.

The people of Laughing Waters village were considering an unusual mid-summer move because of the growing scarcity of game and graze for their horses. Jeremiah felt the spring fed stream near the cabin site would be able to maintain its flow throughout the summer and the grassy stream banks would be ample for his family, but he knew he would have to watch the flow and the weather to ensure their ability to provide the necessary winter supply.

The new cabin was built in the same location as the previous one occupied by Ezekiel and Jeremiah. Using the solid fireplace and chimney built by Ezekiel with his skill and experience from his slave days on the plantation, the new cabin was larger now to accommodate the growing family. With a separate bedroom for Jeremiah and Waters, a loft for Caleb and later to include the new member of the family, the remainder of the cabin was one large room for both table and chairs for the family. With a hard-packed dirt floor, shuttered window openings, and ample chinking between the logs, the cabin promised to be a cozy home for the Thompsetts. With the last cedar shake placed on the roof, the latches on the shutters and doors, it was time for the family to spend their first night in their new home.

Standing outside and admiring their handiwork, Jeremiah reached down and swooped Laughing Waters into his arms to carry her through the doorway. In response to Waters quizzical look, he announced, "I'm carryin' my bride over the threshold! It's an old white man custom, and s'posed ta bring many years' good luck!

Waters giggled as he sat her on the newly made chair in front of the fireplace and smiled as she noted the large cast iron pot hanging from the metal rod over the empty hearth. Standing and clapping her hands as she bounced in a circle to admire the interior of the cabin, she lovingly spoke to Jeremiah, "It will be good here. I believe we will have many happy years for our family. I love you, my husband," and she jumped to put her arms around his neck to give him a lingering hug.

"Hey you two, cut it out. I'm hungry and there ain't nuthin' cookin' so ya ain't got time fer all that nonsense," kidded Caleb, but they all knew he enjoyed everything about being a part of this family and always joined in the fun times as well as the work times. As they enjoyed their first meal in the cabin, they discussed their plans for the coming days. It would soon be necessary to start laying in their winter meat, finish the shelter for the horses, and continue with the education for Caleb.

With his only textbook being Ezekiel's Bible, most of Caleb's learning came from the many stories and guidance offered within the pages of the Holy Book. Many were the times that Ezekiel had instructed Jeremiah using this same Bible and the lessons were well learned. Now

Jeremiah sought to duplicate the process with Caleb. They often shared the reading and the question and answer time with Waters sitting in and learning as well. The rest of Caleb's education took place in the wilderness on a day to day basis. He had proven to be an excellent student and was rapidly becoming an excellent woodsman.

Waters was continually amazed at the boy's ability with the many sounds of the animals and often tried to duplicate what came so easily to Caleb, but her efforts were less than productive. In everything, the family shared their times and learning with one another and enjoyed every day to its fullest. It was a good life.

A MERE WHISPER OF LIGHT CRAWLED OVER THE Eastern horizon in the far distance. Jeremiah sat leaning against a tall Ponderosa at the edge of the clearing that cradled the new cabin. He enjoyed the quiet of early morning and the dim light that hid the scars of both mankind and nature. It had become his habit to greet the dawn of each day, it was a time of gratefulness and communion with his God.

Many of The People, as Water's Arapaho referred to themselves, would greet each day as a time to make offering of pollen and prayers to the Creator. As Jeremiah had learned of this practice, he admonished himself and determined to meet with his Lord each morning as well. He watched as the undersides of the few clouds were slowly painted with the muted colors of early morning. The mountains of the Wind River Range ran from the North West to the South East and with the cabin site in a half-moon clearing that faced the East, the sun readily filled the glade with the brightness of the morning.

As the warmth of the morning sun bathed his full length, Jeremiah stood to return to the cabin and start his day. Waters greeted her husband as he returned to the cabin by showing him her mastery of cooking over the fire in the fireplace. Using the swinging iron arm that normally held the cast iron pot, she draped long strips of fresh venison to drip their juices on the fire below as the dancing flames licked and cooked the red meat.

A Dutch oven sat to the side with its lid covered with hot coals and Jeremiah knew his favorite corn meal biscuits would soon be ready. The aromas of breakfast roused Caleb from his blankets in the loft and as he rose from his slumber, he banged his head on an overhead rafter eliciting a loud, "Ouch! Dang it!" which in turn brought chuckles from the two below. The boy rolled out of his covers with one hand on his forehead, made his way to the ladder, and carefully stepped down to join his adopted parents. Living in the cabin would take some time for each one to become accustomed to the "log teepee" as Waters called their new home.

As they discussed the day over breakfast, they agreed that Waters would return to the village for their remaining possessions and Jeremiah and Caleb would go on a scout and hunt for fresh meat, but to also evaluate the growing drought problem and what game was available. This had proven to be one of the worst times of drought anyone in the village could remember and many had already stated their belief that the game would soon be gone.

Elk herds usually migrated to the high country in the summer months anyway, but with the drought they were not only moving higher but further North. Even the ante-lope and deer that normally preferred the lower eleva-tions and the greener valleys were being forced higher into the mountains. The snow melt from the previous winter usually kept high mountain valleys greener longer into the summer than the lower valleys as the watershed waned.

Jeremiah mounted his steel dust gelding as Caleb swung up into the saddle aboard his strawberry roan. Waters held the lead rope from the pack mule and held it up to her husband as he leaned down and with an arm around her waist, he scooped her up to embrace her with a good-bye hug. Lowering her to the ground, he took the lead rope from her and said, "We should be back about dark, but if not, it'll be because we had to go a bit further than expected, so if you wanna stay at the village for a day or two, we'll see ya' when we get back." Waters smiled and nodded as she peered at her husband, shielding her eyes from the still low hanging morning sun. Taking the obscure high trail that led past the shoulder of the mountain and through a cut in the forest, the two hunters looked back over their shoulders to see Waters still standing in the clearing watching her men depart.

The steel dust had a ground eating gait that prompted Caleb to occasionally gig his roan to a trot to keep up. The mule with his long legs and sure footed walk easily stayed with the lead gelding and always main-tained a disinterested expression with an attitude of aloofness typical of mules. Ever the observant one, Caleb listened to the noises of the forest and whenever he heard the call of a bird, he would answer with a perfect mimicry.

Even the squirrels, chipmunks and other varmints of the forest carried on a conversation with the visitor to their domain. Jeremiah had become so used to the boy's sound effects, he no longer bothered trying to determine which sound was made by the creature and which was made by Caleb. Black Kettle was insightful when he gave the name of Talks with the Wind to the boy. It was not unusual for warriors and white men alike to try to duplicate certain calls of birds and other creatures to aid in their hunting and even as signals in battle, but to the seasoned hunter it was easy to determine the original from the imitation. Caleb's calls, however, were so accurate and realistic it was impossible to tell the difference.

"After we cross this slide rock, we'll hole up on the other side yonder, there's a spring and a bit of graze for the horses so we'll take a break and eat a bite ourselves," informed Jeremiah.

"I was beginning to wonder if we were ever gonna stop," and lifting his eyes heavenward Caleb continued, "after all, it is gettin' on mid-day and I'm gettin' hungry."

"You're always hungry, that's why we have to keep gettin' fresh meat. You're almost as bad as a hungry wolf!" kidded his Uncle.

Crossing a slide rock area was usually difficult due to the very nature of the flat slabs of broken rock that garnered the name, but the sure-footed mounts easily navigated the narrow trail across the steep slide area. With a narrow strip of trees that separated the slide area from the small grassy park and hid the small spring, they followed the trail to the edge of the clearing, dismounted and tethered the mounts. Loosening the cinches and ensuring the lead ropes were sufficient to allow them to water and graze, Jeremiah carried his saddle bags to the shade of the lodgepole pines. Both hunters took a seat on the grassy knoll overlooking the spring and Jeremiah shared several strips of jerky with Caleb.

Ever the teacher and student, it was common for Jeremiah to question or instruct the boy to aid his learning and growth. Now turning to Talks with the Wind, White Wolf said, "So, what have you noticed today on our short jaunt. Anything?"

"Hmmmm. . . well, one thing- there's not the usual numbers of birds and small animals. In country like this, there's almost a continual chatter of calls and stuff, but today there just weren't as many."

"Why do you think that is?" asked the older mountain man.

"I dunno, maybe the drought, the weather, I'm not sure," replied Caleb.

"That was a good observation. You noticed it more than I did, because you're always talkin' to 'em. What else did you notice?"

"Well, it's awfully dry. Even when we crossed pine needles on the trail, when it's usually real quiet movin' on 'em, today they were so dry they were cracklin' like pine cones instead of pine needles. And the branches of the pines seem to be droopin' a little, like they're really thirsty. And even this grass," he said motioning to the normally green grass surrounding the spring, "it's only green right next to the water, and all that out there is turnin' brown. Ain't it too early for that?"

"Yup, you're right. I've never seen it this dry before. Also, usually we would see more sign of game. There weren't any fresh tracks of elk and I only saw one set of deer tracks that crossed the trail. That doesn't look good for our meat supply. And that pool below the spring, it's usually twice that big, but this heat seems to be suckin' the moisture outta everything.

After we cross the park there, the trail takes us over a bit of a saddle and opens up into a nice protected valley that usually holds some elk. We'll stop in the trees and see if we can stalk up on foot and hopefully get something."

They mounted up and resumed their hunt. A quarter of an hour brought them to the edge of the valley and the hunters dismounted to begin their stalk. Tethering the horses back in the trees, the two men checked the loads on their rifles and Jeremiah motioned for Caleb to lead out. Surprised but pleased, the boy stepped off the trail to make his stalk through the thicker lodgepole pines.

Lodgepole pine gained their name by the natives because they grow tall and straight but never big and make great poles for lodges with their small diameter and strength. Now the men often had to turn sideways to move through the thick growth. Nearing the edge of the clearing, they dropped to their knees and peered over the brush at the edge of the meadow. The many chokecherry bushes and intermittent kinnikinnick provided good screen for the hunters to search the meadow for game.

The meadow was empty. This park, about two

hundred yards by three hundred, usually held large numbers of elk and often attracted many predators like wolves and grizzly, but the stunted grass was stiff and brown and the dry breeze held no promise of moisture. Remaining still and searching the tree line, the hunters scanned the entire perimeter again and again searching for any sign of game.

The absence of life in the park prompted the hunters to stand and return to their mounts in silence. As they untied the horses and pack mule, Jeremiah said, "Guess we gotta go higher. This trail will take us up to timberline but we should see something before we get that high. There's a couple more sizable clearings we havta' cross, maybe we'll see somthin' there," he stated to reassure both Caleb and himself.

Another hour brought them to the tree line of the second clearing and the men reined up to view the open area from horseback. Suddenly Caleb swung his leg over the cantle of his saddle and dropped to the ground with rifle in hand. Jeremiah followed suit trusting his nephew had seen something he missed. Then looking in the direction of Caleb's pointed rifle, he spotted three young bull elk walking away from them on a trail across the face of the nearby hillside. At a distance of just over one hundred yards, it would be a decent shot. Dropping to one knee and starting to take aim, he heard Caleb make the repeating grunting sound of a cow elk. The bulls stopped to look in their direction giving the hunters a better shot, Jeremiah said, "I'll take the lead bull, you take that one on the left." The two shots were simultaneous and sounded as one. When the smoke cleared, the men stood to see the bulls. One was trotting away on the trail, while the lead bull was down, and Caleb's bull took two steps, dropped to his knees and fell to his side.

Retrieving their horses and pack mule from the trees, the two hunters made their way to the downed elk to begin butchering. Each one worked on their own kill, skinning out the carcass and stretching it out to bundle the large cuts of meat for packing. Taking the heart, liver, loins and back-straps and the trimmed cuts from the front quarters and hind quarters made bundles of a couple of hundred pounds each. It was a considerable load for the mule, but with the pack frame and balanced bundles, he handled it well. With a few hours of daylight left, they began the return journey home.

THE MERCILESS HOT SUMMER SUN WITHERED THE grasses to brown brittle stubble. Sagebrush, with its customary greenish purple tones, drooped from the normal upright stance under the blaze of the unhindered glare. The azure blue canopy that usually heralded good weather held no clouds. Anything that stirred caused the lazy dust to seek another cooler spot to settle.

Three women and one teenaged girl, all clad in gingham full-length dresses and sun bonnets, trudged beside the wagons. Two men on horseback led the procession of three wagons, each pulled by horses with heads hanging low. The powdered dirt of the trail protested their passing with wisps of dust that grabbed at every passing thing. Without any relief from even a mild summer breeze and no shade to be found, the travelers choked often on the alkaline dust of the central plains of the wilderness territory.

Just after high noon, the wagons turned slightly north and stopped. The little shade from the dirty white canvas bonnets of the wagons provided some relief but each member of this small party dropped and leaned back against the wagon wheels for what little respite was available. Each of the drivers, one older man and two strapping teen boys, climbed down and grabbed the ladle by the water barrels, partially filled buckets and carried water to the horses. Using the ladles, they carried the small allotted portions to each member of their own wagon family. The few sips did little to refresh the tired walkers, but the thought of some relief by their turn in the driver seat gave hope to the women. It had become their routine for the women to walk in the morning, and the men and boys to stretch their legs in the hotter afternoons.

Three days back they crossed the little Powder river and topped off their water barrels but the blistering heat had dwindled their supply. According to the old trapper that directed them this way, they should reach the Wind River in another day. The women had already discussed the decision to take an unproven trail in the hopes of finding a shorter route to the Oregon country, and all three agreed they weren't pleased with the men's decision. But their way was committed and all they could do was take it one step at a time, even though any progress in this heat was begrudgingly yielded.

Five days had passed since they left the North Platte and the rest of the McFadden wagon train and the many friends that chose to stay on in the fertile valley of the North Platte and establish their homes there instead of going on to Oregon. Three families, the Evans, the Walcott's and the O'Reilly's chose to continue mainly due to the old trapper that swore, "Of course, there's a shorter route. Why, ol' Jim Bridger hisself discovered it over three decades ago. Ya just foller the Wind River to its head, turn southwest and go over Union Pass. Been there many times myself."

The women agreed there was enough stubbornness residing in their three husbands to hold back a steam engine. All three had befriended one another from the beginning of this long trip that started almost five months ago. Although different in many ways, the men's determination to go all the way to Oregon bound them together and whenever they gathered around an evening campfire, the talk always focused on what the promised land of Oregon held for their families. In the women's conversations, they were unified in their judgment their men had been born a decade or two too late, as it seemed they would have preferred to be explorers and mountain men instead of Johnny-come-lately settlers. When the women expressed concern about their small numbers and the possibility of Indian attack, they were assured their men would be adequate protection, after all, they were all well-armed and quite capable men.

Resting on the western horizon, the formerly blazing white-hot sun began to blush with brighter shades of orange. With daylight soon to take flight, the travelers turned into a slight cove of protection afforded by a small, flat-topped and rock-rimmed mesa. The three wagons parked in an arc to provide a barrier to keep the animals within the cove. The dropped tongues and closeness of the wagons eliminated the need for either hobbles or tethers on the horses. The animals were glad to be free from their harness and a rubdown with the dried grasses was welcomed by all. The horses worked their way deeper into the cove as they searched for anything that resembled green for graze.

The two men, Walt Evans and Sean O'Reilly, that led the way during the day, had trotted off after some antelope sighted just before the stop. They now returned with one of the tan and white animals across the rump of Sean's horse, and dropped it near the wagon closest to the beginnings of their evening's campfire. The fresh meat would be a welcome addition to the night's fare, but Walter Junior complained, "Prairie Goat again? Man, I'll be glad when we can get some deer or fish or somethin' besides goat! It seems like that's all we've had for weeks!"

The women had taken measure of the young man and knew his verbal assaults were nothing more than his attempts to be like his belligerent father. No one responded to the impudence so he turned and stomped away to find something else to complain about. Just past sixteen, Junior was full grown and could easily pass for a man, except for his high pitched voice and peach fuzz face. However, he was an excellent marksman and did his fair share of work, even with his complaints. Mabel Walcott expressed her concern to the other women about Junior's influence on her two sons, Matthew and Mark, ages twelve and ten, but was always assured they were good boys in their own right and would see through Junior's bravado.

Walter Evans, Walt, was the unofficial leader of the small group. A big man, broad shouldered and built like a blacksmith with a solid foundation; his smile did little to hide the exploring stare through squinted eyes that often bothered anyone that held conversation with him. His manner was domineering and his stubbornness served him well to exert his will on others. His wife, Theresa, was plain and mousy and was only heard to talk around other women when men were absent. She was a "big-boned" woman and appeared able to handle herself in any conflict with anyone except her husband.

Moses Walcott and his wife Mabel came from sturdy farm stock. Both could handle livestock and could easily be pictured following a team plowing a field or pulling stumps on a farm. That was the life they'd left behind in search of a greater land and more fertile soil. Confident they could grow crops just about anywhere, the dream of open vistas and black soil drew them Westward. Together with their two growing boys, Matthew and Mark, they anticipated a large family farm that could serve many generations.

Sean O'Reilly was a hard working Irishman that had worked laying track for the railroads trying to make their way West. The best at swinging a spike maul and driving the spikes for the rails, his bulging muscles of his shoulders and upper arms stretched the fabric of any shirt he wore. Wanting a better life and home for his family, he also fell victim to the dreams of the promised land of Oregon. His wife Clara, and daughter, Clancy Mae, both sported the red hair of the Irish just like Sean. However, the wanderlust that pervaded Clancy Mae made it difficult for Clara and Sean to keep track of her, so they got her a puppy to be her companion. But that puppy was now almost one hundred fifty pounds of shaggy slobbering blackness that never left her side and was her constant companion. No one was allowed near the girl without permission from Two-Bits, her faithful protector.

With all their differences, the families melded together well. The only loners were Junior, who was always trying to tag-along with his father and the men, and Clancy Mae, whose wanderlust kept her and Two-Bits exploring anything and everywhere they could. The difficulty of the trail across the dry prairie land challenged each one, but all were willing to help each other and try to make the journey more tolerable.

The night in the protective cove afforded by the mesa provided a much needed rest, but the anticipated nearness of the Wind River and refreshing water prompted the caravan to stretch out on the designated trail early the next morning. Chasing their own shadows that stretched out before them by the slow rising sun, the absence of clouds promised another day of desolate travel.

It was none too soon when the weary travelers sighted a distant rim of green on the far horizon that quickened their step and the pace of their horses. As they chased the late afternoon sun westward, the encouraged caravan sought the fresh water and shade from the river's side trees. Dropping off a slight slope to the level of the river, it was evident the water that chuckled across the river bottom covered with rounded stones was much lower than usual. The high waterlines on the banks were easily four feet and more above the current level of the slow moving river.

All agreed this would be a rest and recovery stop as they partook of the long-sought shade and cool water. It would take at least a couple of days for the stock and travelers alike to recuperate after the past week of crossing the prairie. From here on for the next week or two, they would be following the river. The presence of nearby water was a welcome thought for everyone.

WELL CONCEALED BEHIND THE CABIN AND OBSCURED by the scrub oak that climbed the lower reaches of the hill shadowing the log home of Jeremiah and his family, was the entrance to a sizable cavern. It was into this cavern that Jeremiah had escaped when the slave catchers attacked and eventually murdered Ezekiel.

The memory of his escape by climbing the natural chimney within the depths of this chasm used for their cache and supply storage, never left him. The terror and frustration he'd felt for himself and his mentor was compounded by his helplessness. The gang of renegades had caused a minor landslide by exploding a powder horn above the cave's entrance that forced Jeremiah to find another way to escape, but also made it impossible to help Ezekiel.

When he had finally freed himself he found his friend shot and burned in the remains of their cabin. Those memories continued to haunt him and ghost-like images now flashed before him as he pushed aside the thick tangle of oak brush to make his way into the now cleared entrance. The cooler temperatures of the cavern made it an ideal place for storing their winter stock of supplies and the racks that were built to hang the meat kept the smoked haunches out of reach of any predators.

The three trips made by both Caleb and his uncle were sufficient for replenishing their supply of winter meat with the recently bagged elk. Although their current stores wouldn't be a full winter's supply, it certainly was a good start. With the recent additions, Jeremiah calculated they would need at least two more elk and maybe a couple of deer. The thought of making a hunting trip down into the lower valleys and trying for a buffalo or two got him to thinking about the savory hump roasts he'd always enjoyed and he knew Waters would appreciate the change of menu as well. *Hmmm, maybe Caleb and I just might have to plan on a jaunt down below before all them buffler dry up and blow away in this here drought.*

———

Astride her Appaloosa mare, Waters rode leisurely homeward. Her visit with family and friends had been enjoyable though, as always, too short. Her saddle bags and parfleche bulged with the miscellaneous clothing and personal items retrieved from their first lodge that would now take their place in the new "log teepee."

The gentle and solitary ride was a time for reflection and Waters indulged herself as her memory wandered the trails of the past. The white tanned, beaded dress that poked out of the parfleche brought the image of her mother, Whispering Winds, before her. Waters pictured the time her mother had presented her with what would be the beginning of her wedding dress and what she'd said at that time.

"Waters, I have sewn and begun the beading pattern with nothing but happiness in my heart, it is now for you to finish as you have the vision for your life. As I was there at the beginning of your life, so too, I began your wedding dress, but it is up to you to make it even more beautiful in the same way you make your life to fulfill your vision."

A smile spread across her dimpled face as she thought how happy her mother would be if she could see the joy that Waters held in her heart and the life she now had with White Wolf. A tear fought for release from the dark eyes of Laughing Waters as she also remembered the time her mother crossed over. Her father, Black Kettle, the village shaman was unable to prevent her mother going although he tried every remedy he knew, but it was her mother's time to go to the Creator. Lifting her eyes to the blue canopy above, Waters let slip a short greeting of thanks to the great Creator for the time she'd had with her mother. *Now I am going to be a mother as well, I hope I will be as good a Mother as mine was.*

The trail opened into the clearing that cradled the newly completed cabin and Waters caught movement to the side of the log structure and was filled with gladness at the sight of the love of her life, Jeremiah. She couldn't remember when she'd first realized she loved this man, as they had spent most of their time together from the age of twelve summers. Remembering when she first saw what she thought of as a gangly and homely-looking white boy, she chuckled to herself as she watched the now lithe and muscular man that approached. *Maybe I always loved him, I have never thought of another since we met. I wonder if he felt the same way?* Her thoughts were interrupted as Jeremiah reached up to lift her from her mount and wrap her in his arms in a welcome home, embrace.

Caleb smiled at the two as he took the saddle bags and parfleche from the Appaloosa and led the horse to the corral at the edge of the clearing. Looking at the other horses and the mule in the corral, Caleb thought of the different parks and clearings they would ride to each day to give the animals time to graze and eat their fill for the day. Each clearing was near a stream or other water source and provided ample graze for the four animals, but it was necessary to choose a different graze each day so as to give ample time for the meadows to replenish the grass.

Responsibility for the animals was one of Caleb's chores but he was often accompanied by either Jeremiah or Waters. Although he liked their company, he also enjoyed the solitude and opportunity to commune with the various creatures of the mountain and to hone his skills as "Talks to the Wind", as his Indian name inferred.

"Did you have a good visit with your people?" asked Jeremiah as he looked down at the woman he held in his arms. Both leaned back at the waist but held each other close. Waters cocked her head to one side and responded, "My people? They are your people, too."

"You know what I mean, your family and others, you know, all the woman stuff," he replied showing exasperation and embarrassment. He knew the only family he had was 'her people' but he still occasionally thought of himself as an outsider.

With a knowing smile she replied, "Yes, I had a good visit and everyone says to give you their greetings. Though we didn't spend much time with the usual talk because all are concerned about the drought. Did you find any game?"

"Yes, we finally downed a couple of lean bull elk. But they're the only ones we saw. Game is really getting scarce and what tracks we did see were all headed higher and further North."

"That's what concerns the people. They are talking of moving the village, of going north to the pointed mountains, or what you call the Absarokas. The blue mountains that are across the valley and far to the north."

"That would be several days' journey and a tough move for everyone, especially since game is so scarce, but it's probably a wise move. Staying here isn't going to be any easier. I was thinking about going down into the valley to try for some buffalo... do you think Broken Shield would want to join us?"

The smile added a sparkle to her eyes as she said, "Yes, I'm sure Shield would want to join us," as she emphasized the 'us' that showed her happiness at being included in her favorite activity, that of hunting with her husband and her brother. She took great pride in her skills as a hunter/ warrior and often excelled even over her brother and husband, much to her delight and their chagrin. Just the thought of the hunt together spread her smile even wider.

"Well, if we're goin' we probly oughta figger on the next day or two, what with the possibility of a move an' all. Whether they stay or go, they'll need meat and we could always use some more. Maybe we can let Caleb ride back to the village and give Shield the word, whatcha think?"

"I think he could go and return if he left right away. We could even get started later today and have the early morning in the valley for the hunt."

Caleb returned to their side just in time to overhear the last bit of the conversation and asked, "Go where and return?"

"To the village to ask Shield to join us for a buffalo hunt down in the valley," answered Jeremiah. "But, you'll need to leave right away. Think you can do it all right?"

"Of course I can, I'm not a little kid!" proclaimed the youngster emphatically.

Between the skirt and the fender of his saddle and under his right leg hung the scabbard that held Caleb's rifle. His powder horn and possibles bag were strapped across his chest that now swelled with pride at being given such an important mission. He watched as Waters tucked a wrap containing his provisions for the day's journey into his saddle bags. She smiled up at him and patted his leg in a gesture of confidence and concern. Jeremiah looked up at the boy now mounted on his strawberry roan and said, "Now, don't get side-tracked and wander off the trail. Just get on to the village and summon Broken Shield and the two of you git on back here 'fore dark, ya' hear?"

"Sure, sure. I unnerstan' uh, Uncle Jeremiah . . . git

there and git back," then with a look of consternation he said, "Say, kin I just start callin' you two Ma an' Pa? Seein' as how ya' really are . . .ya know, my folks an' all. I git tongue tied tryin' ta' call ya' Uncle Jeremiah and I never know fer sure what to call you," nodding his head toward Waters. "It'd be easier ya know, an' I'd like it ifn' I could."

With surprise on their faces and their mouths slightly open, the two turned to each other and smiled. Then turning to Caleb, Waters said, "We would love that, son."

Caleb's spreading smile showed his joy as he replied, "O.K. then, I gotta git." Giving his mount a leg-squeeze and a click of his tongue, he started for the trail leading to the village. Before entering the trees, he turned and waved to his happy family.

THE SAW TOOTH RIDGES OF THE WIND RIVER RANGE rose tauntingly in the south and west and paraded to the northwest with a flirtatious "follow me" demeanor. Slightly north and also pointing to the northwest rose the foothills often called the Owl Creek mountains that led to the granite crags of the Absaroka Range which stood in a parallel parade with the Wind River Range.

The trail for the wagons, as directed by the old trapper, was to lead them between the two towering ranges and eventually over the Union Pass that straddled the Wind River Range. Travel was easier now as they followed the Wind River that meandered through a fertile valley that lay in the shadows of the mountains. Although the current drought had dropped the water level in the river, water was still plentiful and rationing was no longer necessary.

Night camp was more tolerable, even though meat was still a bit scarce and most had grown weary of the continual antelope. Occasionally, the hunters brought in a deer but most were thin and the meat was lean and stringy. Their supplies of potatoes, flour and salt pork had dwindled during their crossing of the desert plains from the North Platte and now the ladies had to improvise with cat-tail root, wild turnips and wild onions. Tempers had again grown short and flare-ups were common.

A black-snake bull whip cracked above the backs of the two strong, bay draft-horses that labored against the traces and the wagon behind them. The bright red hair tangled its curls over the head of Clara O'Reilly as she handled the leads for the big horses. Muttering to herself she said, "Aye, and that worthless Sean O'Reilly better be bringin' me some fresh meat, or he'll for sure be wishin' he had! An' he better button his lip and quit complainin' or I'll be throwin' it to the dawg!"

"What'd ya say, Mum?" asked Clancy Mae, the twelve-year-old spitting image of her mother, as she walked beside the wagon with one hand resting on the back of her big black dog and constant companion, Two Bits.

"Ah, nuthin' me lil' lass, just talkin' to meself," she replied forcing a smile at her daughter. *It's the only way to have an intelligent conversation nowadays,* she thought. It was unusual for the girl to walk alongside the wagon as she was usually exploring further afield as if she and her dog were lonesome pioneers without a care or responsibility to be had. But the terrain they now traipsed through was no different than the previous several weeks, with endless sagebrush and brittle brown prairie grass and scattered patches of prickly pear and cholla cactus. The trail was straighter than the river bed and the river was now more than a mile distant. When they were closer to the river and more trees and brush, Clancy Mae and Two Bits loved to wander the smaller game trails in search of a rabbit or chipmunks.

Walt Evans and Sean O'Reilly had stretched out in front of the wagons to scout the trail and hopefully scare up some game before the noisier wagons and teams came along. Walt Junior had taken a game trail toward the river and had dropped out of sight behind a small flat-top bluff. The afternoon heat was taking its toll on the scouts and their mounts when suddenly a big-footed and lop-eared jack rabbit jumped from behind a nearby sage brush and sought to out-run the coyote in hot pursuit. Both horses shied and jumped but were soon brought under control as neither horses nor riders had enough excess energy to make much of the slight scare.

"What was that?!? If that was a rabbit, that hadta be the biggest one I ever saw! Did you see them ears?" shouted Sean as he turned to look at Walt.

"He's a big 'un all right. That musta been one o' them thar Jackrabbits that ol' trapper was tellin' us about. I think they also call 'em snowshoes, cuz o' thar big back feet. You'd think he'd make a meal, but it 'pears he ain't nuthin' but feet 'n ears," chuckled the loud Walt.

The rolling and dipping terrain of the valley allowed the scouts to disappear in a low swale then rise to a slight knoll and give a wider field of vision throughout the valley. As they stopped for a look-see, they scanned the slightly greener growths nearer the river and realized the river made a bend back to the northeast and the trail and river would soon intersect again.

The men agreed this would be a good location for the night's camp and gigged their horses in that direction. As they dropped off the knoll, a gunshot rattled and echoed back from the distant bluffs. The sound was coming from nearer the river, and they thought it must be Junior taking a shot at a deer or something. But when that shot was followed by two more, fear showed in Walt's eyes and he spurred his horse to a lope in order to close the distance to his son.

A low area clear of brush and trees at the edge of the river revealed the standing mount and Junior in a one-knee stance preparing to shoot again. When a quick glance in the direction the young man was aiming at revealed nothing but a stirring cloud of dust, Walt yelled,

"What in thunder are you shootin' at, boy?" His horse slid to a stop and he swung his leg over the cantle of his saddle dropping to the ground with rifle in hand. The boy lowered his rifle and pointed with his left hand in the direction of the dust cloud.

"Buffalo! There was a small bunch of 'em, maybe fifteen or so cross the river thar. I guess they was too fer. I couldn't hit any of 'em, they started runnin' at the first shot and was gone before I could get one," he answered disgustedly. "Sorry, Pa, I thought I could get us some good meat. But they're probably clean on back to the North Platte by now."

The leader of the wagon train stomped around and kicked up almost as much dust as the retreating buffalo, all the while muttering and mumbling to himself, "I reckon if ya want sumpin' done right, ya just gotta do it yerself! Ain't nobody 'roun' here worth the powder to blow thar nose!" Then turning to the big Irishman and his son, he said, "Whyn't the two of you mount up n' find us a campsite fer tonight. I'll go on over t other side of the river there n' see if the boy drew blood on anything."

With a wave of his hand, he straddled his mount and pushed him down the bank to cross the shallow river. As his big sorrel rose from the gurgling waters they mounted the low bank and went directly to the churned up soil that had been the beds of the buffalo. Walking his horse in a zig-zag pattern across the many tracks of the small herd, there was no evidence of hide or blood that would indicate his son had scored a hit.

He followed the trail for over a mile as the buffalo took a direct path across the rolling hills seeking another place of graze and water. Nothing about the trail gave Walt the impression the buffalo were going to slow their progress any time soon, so he turned his mount to return to the camp site for the night.

The brightness of the afternoon sun had yielded to scattered clouds that appeared to be snoozing on the mountain tops to the West and now appeared as a bright orange orb that sought to rest from the day's labor and join the darker clouds in slumber. The rattle of trace chains and low rumbling grunts of the draft horses signaled the arrival of the wagons and the families of the scouts and others.

Using the river bank and the nearby trees as a partial shelter, the three wagons formed a half circle to complete the camp. While the men unharnessed the horses, Junior and the two boys led the saddle horses to the edge of the river for water and were soon joined by the men and the rest of the stock. The women busied themselves with the evening meal preparation and Clancy Mae wandered the trees and bushes along the bank in search of small game or edible plants to supplement the meal. Two Bits led the way and the girl soon bagged two rabbits with her handy sling shot.

She had become more adept with the sling as the need became dire. She also dug a bag full of cattail roots and sprouts to complete the evening fare and started to return to show her Mum her bounty. Two Bits froze and let a low murmuring growl emit from his deep chest. Clancy knew not to move or doubt her dog and crouched low beside him. Two Bits put his head down to the trail that led to the water and sniffed at a track, then looked to the river and back from the bushes toward the disappearing hills.

Sniffing the track, then the air, he turned to Clancy and with open mouth he began to pant giving a sign of relief. Clancy stepped forward to look at the track, *That's a moccasin track and ain't none of our'n been thisa way. I bet that's from an injun.* She stood and looked around like Two Bits, then stepped out to return to the campsite.

As she trotted back to the wagons, her mind took its own path in many different directions seeking an answer to her dilemma and fear. She didn't want to scare her Mum and her Da wouldn't want to believe her.

Maybe if I go to Mr. Evans, he is, after all, supposed to be the leader. Maybe he'd listen, but Junior would probably just make fun of me like he usually does. But somebody needs to know... maybe Mr. Walcott. Yeah, I'll tell him, he'll listen to me. The weight of decision and responsibility lifted from her shoulders. Clancy Mae dropped the rabbits and cattail roots next to the campfire and started for the Walcott wagon. When she saw Moses Walcott visiting with his wife, she cleared her throat and said, "Excuse me, Mr. Walcott, could I talk to you a minute? I need to show you somethin' ta see if you know what it is."

The big farmer could see the serious cut to the girl's expression and smiled at his wife and said, "Sure kiddo, I'll take a look at whatever your mystery is."

"It just over here on the trail in the trees a bit, it'll just take a minute."

As she knelt beside the track and pointed, Moses bent down to examine the trail. He walked beside the tracks to the river bank, saw where the moccasin wearer had knelt to scoop a handful of water, then waded across the river. Walking back to the girl, he said, "Well, it looks like there was just one, and he headed on up into the mountains. So, I don't think we got anything ta worry 'bout. I'll let the others know, but don't go blabbin' 'bout this to the womenfolk. We don't wanna get them all upset, y'hear?"

Clancy Mae stood with a smile on her face and nodded her agreement to Moses. "I kinda thot the same thing, that's why I didn't tell my Mum and Da. So, I'll just let you take care of it now, O.K.?"

"Sure kiddo, I don't think there's anything to worry 'bout. They's just as many friendly injuns as bad'uns, an' this'n has already headed for the high lonesome. So, I'm sure we'll be all right."

The two confidants returned to the wagons and the

soon to be ready evening meal. Clancy Mae was looking forward to the rabbit stew and a good long night's sleep. Resting her hand on the big head of Two Bits, she quickened her step to keep up with the long-legged stride of Moses Walcott.

She felt relieved and even proud that Mr. Walcott had come to the same conclusion regarding the moccasin tracks by the river. She secretly hoped she would never see another moccasin track, at least one made by an Indian, again. The many stories she overheard around the late night campfires about the scary things some Indians did to their captives, made it sometimes difficult to sleep through the night. She knew Two Bits would protect her, but there was still the unknown.

THE CAVALCADE OF TRAVELERS NUMBERED THREE hunters and five mounts. They were led by Jeremiah on his steel dust gelding and leading the pack mule followed by Broken Shield on his black and white paint gelding and leading a tall bay pack-horse with Caleb trailing behind on his strawberry roan.

The hopeful band of hunters made their way down the steep mountainside trail in the early morning light. The narrow path was treacherous under any conditions as it switched back on itself to allow the travelers to descend to the narrow ravine below. The Popo Agie Creek snaked its way between two opposing mountains as it carved its way to the valley beyond.

Upon reaching the bottom of the ravine, the hunters followed the creek-side trail past the overhanging cliff that allowed the stream to disappear beneath the granite faced wall. Almost one hundred yards down the rock-strewn ravine the stream mysteriously reappeared from under the cliffs and boulders at the base of the northern mountain on the opposite side of the ravine. The mysterious phenomenon was call The Sinks and was often considered a mystical place by many of the ancients.

The ravine between the mountains began to open allowing the hunters to enjoy the vista of the valley below. The green snake of willows and grass that escorted the descending stream was made vivid by the surrounding browns of the withered sagebrush and brown brittle prairie grass. The brilliance of the morning sun bathed the entire valley in the promise of another blistering, dry day.

Dust devils did the dance of demons as they twisted their hips like dancers in a bizarre and taunting prelude to death. Early morning was the favored time for animals to seek water and graze before the heat of the day would drive them to the cool shade, but there was no evidence of life stirring anywhere near the solitary stream.

Dismounting and walking to the crest of a nearby shoulder of stone, the hunters sought a higher promontory to provide a panoramic view of the valley below. In the shadow of an overhang, the three scanned the valley and focused on the greenery of the Popo Agie banks.

Caleb was the first to speak, "There!" as he shielded his eyes with his right hand and extended his left hand to point to the wide curve of the stream. The dark spots near the tall cottonwoods began to stir as several buffalo casually strolled to the stream side for their morning drink.

"Ah, the Great Spirit smiles on us today," praised Broken Shield as he placed his hand on the shoulder of the boy.

"Well, we don't have them yet, but it sure looks promising," speculated Jeremiah. He immediately formulated a plan for the trio as all three mounted up to pursue the mountainous beasts. Shield and Caleb would swing wide along the broken terrain to the east and come toward the buffalo from the east while Jeremiah would mirror their moves and approach from the west. Shield was shouldered with the responsibility of coordinating the attack.

The next hour passed slowly for Caleb, who was excited about this hunt. Although he had downed most other kinds of meat animals, this would be his first buffalo. Most of the Arapaho and other Native peoples considered a successful buffalo hunt a rite of passage into manhood and Caleb sought the respect of completing that rite.

He had been cautioned by Jeremiah regarding the smaller caliber of his rifle and the need for an appropriate load for his weapon to be effective against the larger buffalo. Accuracy and location of his shot also swirled through his mind as his excitement and anticipation rose to new heights. Hand signals from Shield caught Caleb's attention and they dismounted to tether their mounts before beginning a stalk.

Jeremiah was shielded behind a cluster of boulders several yards away from the grassy area where the buffalo now grazed. His stalk had been unseen and the animals moved lazily, seeking the next green sprouts for their browse. Shield and Caleb worked their way through the scattered willows and kinnikinnick bushes. Within a few minutes both were situated with Shield using a cottonwood sapling as a leaning rest and Caleb took a one-knee stance for his shot.

Talks to the Wind put the front blade of his sight just behind the front shoulder of a young bull with his face in the cluster of grass. A quick hand signal from Shield told Jeremiah they were ready. They had agreed that Shield would take the first shot and as his rifle roared and spit a cloud of white smoke, the other two hunters let loose their messengers of death. The three rifles belched a chorus of thunder that caused a simultaneous jerk of all the animals in the small herd. Heads raised and feet formed a stance of attack or flee.

Turning in unison, the animals began to flee to the riverside to make their escape. Two animals stumbled and fell while the hunters quickly reloaded their rifles. Dropping the powder down the barrels and placing the patch across the muzzles, the accompanying ball was rammed home with the ramrods that were quickly extracted to ready the weapons. This was an action of habit and allowed the hunters to keep one eye on the herd to prepare their next attempt at making meat. The young bull that had taken Caleb's bullet into his side, stumbled and turned to seek out it's assailant.

Dropping his head and reaching out with his front hoof, the huge beast scratched the earth and brought a small cloud of dust and dirt over his back. He blew snot from his nose and bellowed as he started his charge toward the boy. Shield had fired his second charge into the side of a slow moving cow and he now dropped the butt of his rifle beside his left foot to begin his reload.

He saw the bull begin his charge and looked to Caleb

as the boy lowered the barrel of his rifle to bring his sights to bear on the charging animal. As the barrel came down, Caleb brought the hammer to full cock. As his rear buckhorn sights aligned with the front blade centered on the chest of the charging beast, he set the rear trigger and moved his finger to the narrow front trigger. Taking a deep breath and letting a bit out, he slowly squeezed off his shot.

The .38 caliber ball parted the beard on the bull and buried itself deep between the chest muscles to stop the heart of the enraged animal. As the front legs buckled under him, the nose of the bull hit the dust and its head skidded on the mass of fur on its forehead as the animal slid to a stop less than six feet in front of Talks to the Wind.

The boy stood tall and with the brass butt-plate of his rifle resting on the toes of his moccasin, he began to reload. A broad smile spread across the face of Shield as he completed the reload of his own weapon. He shook his head as he thought, *I have never seen a young man that had so much confidence and bravery at that age.*

The herd of wooly brown beasts had splashed their way across the creek and made good their escape following the western bank of the descending stream. On the grassy patch of graze lay the carcasses of five animals that summoned the hunters to the bloody task of dressing the beasts. Both Jeremiah and Shield had dropped two cows each while the lone young bull was Caleb's trophy.

Retrieving their mounts, the men set to work by using the mule to roll the buffalo first to one side and then the other as they stripped the hides from the stubborn carcasses. They continued to labor at the bloody task well into the day, with the only break taken for the noon meal. All three were covered with blood past their elbows and across their middles and the fronts of their britches.

After completing the grisly work, they would bathe, clothes and all, in the nearby stream. Occasionally, each one would have to walk to the stream for a refreshing wash off and deep drink in an attempt to assuage the smell of death. When Caleb sought the relief of the stream, he stood to turn back to his task and noticed a rising cloud of dust in the distance. As he squinted his eyes to improve his vision, his right hand to his forehead, he began to identify the cause of the dust.

"We've got company coming," he quietly spoke to the others. Both men quickly rose to see the cause for alarm and walked to Caleb's side to view the object of concern.

"That's a string of animals, and I count, at least, two men. Looks like white men," stated Jeremiah as he turned to look at Shield. Both men knelt to wash their hands and faces and with a nod, Shield picked up his rifle and disappeared in the nearby brush and trees. Jeremiah motioned for Caleb to join him by the larger of the downed animals and with rifles near at hand, both bent to resume their task. Within a quarter hour, a pack train of five mules accompanied by two men mounted on horses, one leading and one at the rear, pulled to a halt on the opposite side of the stream.

"Hello thar! Mind if we step down and get us a little o' that water?" inquired the whiskered leader of the train.

"Help yourself," replied Jeremiah as he kept his left hand on his weapon.

Both men dismounted leaving their rifles in the scabbards on the far side of their mounts, an obvious sign of trust and peaceful intent. Leading the several animals to the stream, the men kept a grip on the lead ropes of the animals and renewed the conversation with Jeremiah.

"Mind if we make camp over thar? There seems to be more shade and it looks like more graze. We're just a pack train of traders makin' our way thru hyar. If ya'll need sumpin', we probly got it. Ain't done much tradin' so fer, so we're still purty well stocked."

"Come ahead on, I reckon it'll be all right," replied Jeremiah.

As the traders finished watering their stock, they waded the stream and tethered each animal with ample lead rope to enable each one to graze the scattered grasses. The hunters' mounts were tethered nearer the taller cottonwoods slightly downstream from the crossing leaving ample room for the additional animals. After preliminary discussions revealed the hunters plan to start back home without spending the night at the butcher site, the traders began making their camp for the night.

With a casual stroll from the trees, Broken Shield made his presence known as he joined Jeremiah at the grisly task. The older of the two traders also joined the hunters as they continued the work on the fourth of the five buffalo.

"Would you fellers be interested in a little tradin' fer some of them hides?" inquired the trader. "By the way, muh name's Pickles, it's a handle I picked up while I wuz trappin' fer the American Fur comp'ny up on the

Musselshell. My partner over yonder's muh nephew, Samuel. This is his first time out chere."

"My handle's Jeremiah, an' this here's Broken Shield of the Arapaho, and the squirt over there is my son, Caleb." Standing and turning to look at the bow-legged pot-bellied old trapper, Jeremiah asked, "I ain't never seen anybody try tradin' with just a pack train. Most usually come with a bunch o' wagons and such. Whatever prompted you to try this?"

"Wal, what with the rendezvous with the bigger companies not happenin' anymore, I figger there's still a few left out here that ain't got much ta trade but still need some supplies. So, I thot it'd give me a chance to see the mountains agin, and give the boy there a 'xperience of a lifetime. You fellers needin' anything? I could use a couple them hides if yore of a mind to part with 'em."

Although the buffalo hides were prized and needful, they were also extremely heavy before curing and tanning. With only two pack animals and meat from five buffalo, the idea of trading a couple of hides for some additional supplies appealed to the hunters. After Shield told Jeremiah of Caleb's need of putting two bullets into the young bull before he dropped, Jeremiah's previous thoughts of the necessity of a larger caliber rifle for Caleb were renewed. And so the trading began. When all the dickering and bartering was complete, the traders load was lightened by flour, cornmeal, sugar, galena and percussion caps, and a good supply of black powder. Caleb was involved in the trade of his .38 caliber percussion Kentucky rifle for a .54 caliber Hawken and walked away with a puffed out chest and talking to himself about his new rifle.

With the long-legged mule packing the greatest load, Shield's pack horse loaded high, and each of the hunter's carrying supplies or cuts of meat in their saddle bags and parfleche's, the hunters pointed their mounts for return to the mountains. It would be near dark- or after- before the group would gain sight of the Log Teepee in the clearing, but the rising moon provided ample light for the rest of the trip. When they arrived at the clearing, dark was just settling over the tall pines, yet Waters stood in the lighted doorway to greet the returning hunters. Temporarily placing the packs with the meat in the cavern, the men walked back to the cabin to turn in for the night. Caleb proudly carried his new Hawken over his shoulder as he walked to the door.

"Say Pa, can we go out an' do some shootin' with my new Hawken tomorrow?" asked the boy as he trailed the men to the cabin.

"Well, I dunno, did you see that lightning out east there? We might get some much needed rain tomorrow and it's kinda hard to do any shootin' with wet powder."

"Aw, we've seen lightnin' before an' it never amounted ta' nuthin'. All we got wuz just a couple a raindrops an' a whole lotta noise!"

"Yeah, I know, but that's startin' to shape up like more of a storm than usual. It might be a gully washer. What do you think Shield?" asked Jeremiah.

Turning to look at the distant lightning and listening to the low rumble of faraway thunder, Shield responded with, "I don't smell rain, mebbe just lightning and thunder," as he stepped to the door of the cabin.

The hunters were welcomed with a venison stew in the hanging pot over the coals of the fire in the fireplace and each consumed an ample amount. Caleb spent more time telling Waters about the hunt and the new rifle than eating but as the chatter subsided, he made up for lost time. With the long day behind them, the four turned in for a much needed night's sleep.

THE GREY GRANITE FINGERS SCRATCHED AT THE brilliant blue of the afternoon sky. It appeared as if the devil himself had thrust his bony claws through the mountain top in a futile effort to reach heaven. Below the bony digits lay a mantle of blue timber with slashes of white glaciers capping the summer shades of pine.

Clara O'Reilly once again found herself in sole command of the land yacht being dragged Westward by the slow-plodding draft horses. Every step of the big hooves raised a small cloud of dust in protest of the disturbance. The fine grains of powdered adobe and alkali settled in her uncovered crown of Irish Red curls and drifted lazily over her gingham dress.

She had grown too tired to bother with wiping her prairie gown free from the hitchhikers. She lifted her eyes to the stony crags that threatened to snag the first clouds that dared to pass by and marveled at the wonder of God's creation. She thought to herself, *If circumstances were a bit different, I might even enjoy this country. It reminds me of the glens of Ireland with a mighty tall frame surrounding the beauty below.* This was the fourth day since they first crossed the Wind River and began the leg of their trip that would lead them to the shortcut to Oregon over the mysterious Union Pass. Sean, her big strapping Irishman of a husband, had joined Walt Evans to scout the trail in search of the Union Pass turnoff. Clara reminisced over the last fifteen years; the voyage from Ireland, the years as indentured servants, meeting Sean and running off together, and most pleasantly, the birth of their only child, Clancy Mae. Their twelve-year-old daughter had been a wonder from the day of her birth. Always curious, never afraid, independent and, of course, stubborn like every red-headed lassie Clara ever knew.

A snort and uplifted head from her team brought Clara from her reverie and focused her attention on an approaching rider, her husband. With a wave of his hat, he signaled the wagons to pull nearer the tree line and stop for the nooning. Clara complied with a shake of the lead lines that bounced on the rumps of her team and a strong pull to the right brought the wagon into the shade of the tall pines.

As Sean rode near the wagon he spoke to Clara, "I think we've located the turnoff for Union Pass. We should make it at least near there by tonight and get an early start in the morn. Plus, there's good fresh water and plenty of graze to fatten up the horses. We might e'en stay an extry day ta' rest up." His smile spread through the thick red beard and revealed a row of white teeth in contrast to the whiskers. He knew his wife and the rest of the women could use a day to rest up and catch up on chores like washing clothes and bathing the kids and more.

Clara responded, "Now don't go kiddin' me, Sean Michael O'Reilly. You know I need a rest day an' if you're just gonna tell me 'bout it and take it away, it's a big scallywag ye are."

"I'm not kiddin' woman. You'll get your rest day, ne'er fear."

Mable Walcott and Theresa Evans were walking together toward the O'Reilly wagon when they heard the 'rest day' comment and asked in unison, "Rest day? Really?"

"Yes ladies, but not till we get to the turnoff later today, maybe 'bout sundown."

The news was well received and the ladies quickly returned to their wagons to get the noon meal finished so they could get back on the trail. It was the first time in many days that anyone was anxious to get on the move again, but the idea of a rest day gave a welcome dose of optimism to the entire group. The noon meal consisted of antelope jerky and leftover breakfast cornmeal biscuits all washed down by some fresh Wind River water.

The much needed rest for the horses allowed for minimal graze and a welcome drink, but the teams were soon hooked back to the wagons that groaned and creaked in protest as the small train was again on the move. Theresa Evans pulled her wagon into the lead and followed the trail that wound through the sagebrush and scattered cactus patches. At times, the trail was a two-track that looked as if wagons had preceded them, and other times it looked like nothing but wild animals made a path to find water at the river's edge. But the progress continued, though slow and often meandering.

Clancy Mae was up to her usual escapades wandering around in the nearby trees and bushes with her faithful companion, Two Bits. With a seemingly inexhaustible source of energy, the precocious adolescent would explore the nearby woods, then pop her head out to keep track of the wagons, and occasionally stalk the slow moving caravan and jump out to startle her Mum and elicit a playful, "Oh you! You keep that up and you'll scare me right into old age! Now come up here an' give your Mum a hug."

And without missing a step the child would bound up with a foot on the stub of a shelf with the water barrel, and vault into the seat beside her mother to retrieve the promised hug. But within moments, she would join her best friend, Two Bits, on another excursion into the wilderness, often returning with a rabbit for the pot that had been caught by Two Bits or dropped with a stone from her sling-shot.

———

Barcheeampe, or Pine Leaf, was the Bacheeitche or war leader of the Eelalapito Crow. A sub-group of the Crow nation, the Kicked in the Bellies group claimed the area surrounding the Absaroka Mountain Range and south to the Wind River Range as their territory. Although they did not view property ownership like the white man, it was their land to live and hunt and anyone that entered this land was considered an enemy. Pine Leaf sat astraddle of her sorrel stallion and with head and shoulders erect she exuded her authority as war leader.

The three warriors beside her looked through the sparse pines on the rocky escarpment to watch the slow progress of the wagons. Pine Leaf was a fearless warrior and had earned her position as war leader or pipe carrier by the many feats performed in battle with both white men and enemy tribes like the Arapaho, Blackfeet and Gros Ventre.

She brandished the scalp locks on her shield and lance and the feathers worn in her long black braids were badges of honor. The fierce warrior was also a stunningly beautiful woman that any man would treasure as a mate, but she chose to ride alone. The stern expression that covered her countenance told her warrior companions what would soon take place, with eyes that flared with anger and malevolence and a down-turned mouth, her rigid features spoke of a coming battle.

When much younger, Barcheeampe would freely wander the woods near her village without fear of any danger. She felt confident in her abilities with the bow against any animal of the woods, but she never thought of the danger that trapped her in the muscular arms of a dirty white trapper and his partner. They man-handled her, taking her from her village to their camp and ravaged her body, muting her screams and fighting off her struggles until they sated their lust. As the monstrous men snored in their buffalo robes, Pine Leaf wore her arms raw as she twisted herself free of her bonds and escaped.

Returning to her lodge, she retrieved her bow and

quiver of arrows without speaking to anyone, then made her way back to the trapper trash and their camp. While they still snored, she buried the shafts of three arrows into each chest and belly in rapid succession as the drunken louts struggled to free themselves from their robes. From that time forward, she sought vengeance on any and all white men that dared to invade their territory. This group would soon feel her wrath and contempt as she impaled them on her arrows and lance without mercy.

With a nod to her men, they turned their horses back toward their camp where more warriors waited in anticipation for another opportunity to decorate their lodges with the scalps of the hated white men. Twelve more warriors, some young and inexperienced and others proven in battle, awaited their war leader. She had many times led them into battle and all were eager to prove themselves to their honored battle chief.

———

The western edge of the valley was bordered with tall Douglas fir and Engleman spruce on the furthermost bank of the Wind River. At these upper reaches of the Wind River valley, the stream had carved its course nearer the edge of the mountainside that towered over the fertile but narrow plain below. Walt Evans and Sean O'Reilly walked their mounts nearer the river bank in search of a good campsite for the night. Their chosen location was just below the trail that turned to mount the sloping hillside and cut between the two larger mountains and was undoubtedly the cutoff for Union Pass as blazed by none other than Jim Bridger himself.

The men sat astride their mounts and the horses dropped their heads for a long drink of refreshing water. The whispers of death assaulted them before they knew they were in danger. Both men looked down to see the feathered shafts that protruded from their chests and felt another pair of arrows bury themselves alongside the first. With only an instant to look at one another, both men slid from their mounts and rolled down the gravelly bank to come to rest at the water's edge. Blood drained from their lifeless bodies and colored the otherwise crystal clear stream.

Several warriors quickly appeared and retrieved the mounts, led them into a clearing away from the trees and tethered them to ground stakes. The mounts would be easily seen by the approaching wagons and the group of travelers would assume the men were in the shade or nearby. Others dragged the bodies into the brush, scalped them, and hastily covered them with brush, twigs and leaves. Within moments, the tranquil scene appeared undisturbed and the men's mounts grazed lazily at the edge of the shady meadow.

Less than a half hour later, the wagons approached the anticipated campsite. The trail had closely followed the river and was often in the shade of the nearby trees and the task of keeping the horses moving instead of dropping their head to snatch a mouthful of grass had become rather tedious so the women were anxious to make their camp. Stopping the wagons in the usual half circle using the trees as a shelter, the women started to dismount and start their chores.

Theresa Evans was the first to feel the pang of death as a warrior's arrow buried itself between her breasts, causing her to miss her step and fall face first to the ground and breaking off the shaft, but Theresa was beyond feeling. Junior, still mounted beside the wagon, saw his mother fall but didn't see the arrow. As he leaned toward the seat of the wagon, an arrow whistled by his head and pierced the white canvas of the wagon. Junior dropped back into his saddle and grabbed for the rifle contained in the scabbard beneath his right leg. He quickly brought it up, cocked the hammer and fired at a charging and yelling warrior that was coming fast with an upraised tomahawk.

The red blossom on the young warrior's chest stopped the charge as his legs gave way and he caved to the ground. Bringing his rifle down to his side, Junior fumbled for his powder horn and possibles bag, but was surprised to see blood dripping onto his hands, then he felt the tomahawk that was buried in his head and the blackness of death covered his eyes.

Moses Walcott saw Theresa Evans fall from the seat of her wagon and he also saw the feathered shaft protruding from her chest. With a yell to his wife to "Get the boys, and git down!" he retrieved his double-barreled shotgun from beside the seat and leveled it at a screaming banshee charging on horseback with a lance poised to strike.

The first barrel's load wiped the face from the Indian's head and bloodied his neck and shoulders as he slumped to the neck of his now, spooked horse. Within two steps behind the first warrior followed another on foot with an arrow notched in his bowstring. Stopping to lift the arrow toward the burly man on the wagon, he received the second barrel's load of misery and his chest and belly melted in a mass of blood and tissue. Motion and life stopped in that instant for the warrior seeking his first feather.

Feeling the nudge at his elbow, Moses handed his shot gun to his wife to reload and took the Kentucky rifle from her grip in time to plant a .54 caliber slug in the neck of another painted and screaming warrior. Starting to hand the rifle back to his wife, he felt the mass of blood on the seat and turning, saw the pooling blood running from the scalped head of his beloved wife. He turned quickly to see the bloody knife of a warrior plunge into his side and twist to bring a spring of blood to join his wife's. Before his eyes closed in death, he saw the bodies of his two boys sprawled against the sides of the wagon, sightless eyes staring upwards and blood still running from their slit throats.

The fiery red hair and screaming curses that emanated from Clara O'Reilly gave the charging warriors pause, enough so that she was able to empty the two barrels of her shotgun into the mid sections of two warriors that stood transfixed at the color of her hair and the freckled countenance that spewed such venom. With no other weapons, she taunted them to come at her but her challenge was silenced when a lance soared over the heads of the warriors and into the chest of the mad Irishwoman.

Looking down at the ridiculous protrusion, she lifted her eyes to see that a woman was the one who launched the instrument of death into her body. Pine Leaf watched as the big red-head looked at her with a confused expression on her face. Clara thought, *That's a woman. A woman's not supposed to do that. Why . . .?* and fell from her stand in her wagon to land in death in the dust.

Watching from the trees and behind some willows, Clancy Mae knelt with an arm around Two Bits and quieted him with a whispered warning in his ear. *We can't do nuthin' Two Bits, we just gotta stay hid, so them injuns don't find us. Shhhh .... quiet now.*

THE SKELETAL WHITE FINGERS OF THE LIGHTNING clawed at the black velvet of the night sky like a macabre phantom of the netherworld seeking to escape the chains of eternity. The clap of thunder that heralded the light show in the Southern sky seemed to shake the needles from the dry pines that crawled up the mountainside to flee the fire in the sky. As the darkness of the night deepened, the creatures of the night sky walked their way up the valley to the accompanying drums of rolling thunder.

Every tentacle of lightning that reached down to the dry terrain was mirrored time and again as the image was duplicated in rapid succession across the wide expanse of darkness. The animals in the corral near the cabin grew restless as they paced the small enclosure shoulder to shoulder and murmured to one another with muted whinnys drawn from deep in their nervous chests. Each roll of thunder would startle the horses, driving them to the opposite side of the corral and the next flash of lightning would chase them to the back of the shelter. Each collision with the pole fence weakened the structure that moaned and squeaked with every strain.

The restless animals brought Jeremiah for a look-see at the ruckus. Concerned about some predator, he was surprised at the fury of the encroaching lightning storm. Leaning with one foot on the bottom rail of the fence, he sought to calm the horses with low words of encouragement. He was surprised to hear Shield behind him as he said, "Bad storm, lightning but no rain. Could cause some fire."

"That's for sure. These dry storms can sure make a mess o' things, especially since everything's so dry. So far, I don't see any sign of fire though. Maybe we'll be lucky an' nuthin'll happen but just a bunch a' noise. Course, that makes it mighty hard ta' git some sleep."

"Hah! People die in their sleep. It's not that important anyway," kidded Shield.

Although closer, the storm was still a considerable distance away and seemed to be mostly in the lower valley. The two friends continued to observe the storm and calm the horses for several minutes before agreeing to return to the cabin and get the much needed rest. Entering the cabin, they were surprised to see Waters pouring both men a fresh cup of coffee at the table and smiling as they sat opposite of one another. Waters poured herself one and joined the two for a middle of the night visit. Jeremiah noticed how Waters buckskin dress was becoming tighter around her midriff, evidence of the blossoming pregnancy. Unlike white women, being with child did little to slow the work and activity of the Indian.

"Is that storm going to give us any rain, or is it just going to argue with the gods?" asked Laughing Waters.

"Well, usually with as much light as its givin' off we could see any rain comin' but it sure doesn't appear to be anythin' but thunder and lightning. Course, ol' big nose here, " he said as he nodded toward Shield, "thinks he could smell any rain if there was some, but he says there ain't no rain."

"It's sure that you can't smell anything 'cause your nose is full of the smell of your woman," retorted Broken Shield with a broad smile.

"Umm Humm ..." replied Jeremiah as he leaned over to nibble on Waters ear, causing a giggle to escape from the woman.

To change the subject a little, Waters asked the men, "Do you think the corral will hold the horses if the storm gets any closer?"

"I think so, they've settled down some and if it gets any worse we'll go out there again to make sure they don't get too spooked. Don't want to have to go chasin' 'em down if we don't have to," answered the mountain man.

As they nursed their coffee, the conversation turned to the drought, meat supplies, and the coming winter. Although some months away, much of the time during the warmer months was spent preparing for the harsh winters that often assailed the mountains and made survival a challenge. The meat secured from the recent buffalo hunt still required a lot of work in smoking and curing for the preservation of the precious resource. They would normally be able to supplement their supply with the many plants of the area like turnips, cat-tail roots, berries and other natural foods used by the people of the mountains, but the drought had dwindled the usual bounty.

Knowing the sun would soon chase away the darkness, the three friends chose to try again to catch the elusive sleep they needed before the work of the coming day. Waters and Jeremiah went to their room as Shield returned to his blankets on the floor near the fireplace. The sounds of sleep soon drifted through the warm cabin.

Over four miles away and at the downhill edge of the black timber, a large branch of the skeleton of white light drove itself down the length of the towering ponderosa pine splitting it into shreds of yellow bark and scattering a shower of sparks in a wide circle about the base of the ragged stump. The dry pine needles that formed a mattress of tinder around the base began to smolder and suddenly hungry flames licked up to consume the crispy dry fare. Within moments, the growing flames stretched across the few feet that separated the ponderosa from the nearby blue spruce and the fiery monster began to climb the trees like a hungry boy after a ripe apple.

Climbing the stump to consume the volatile pitch, the flames now stretched to the heights of both trees and sought the outstretched branches of the neighboring and assorted dry pines. Aided by the storm caused wind that blew from the valley and climbed to the mountaintops, the flames began to jump from tree-top to tree-top and within moments the small cluster of flames became a raging inferno being swept up the mountainside with ever increasing hunger. Two ridges separated the growing fire from the Arapaho village nestled on the slight plateau at the shoulder of the higher mountains, and a third ridge and long draw made the distance to the cabin a short ride. But these hindrances were inconsequential to the all-consuming monster of flames that began to stalk the unsuspecting Arapaho sleeping in their buffalo hide teepees and brush hut shelters.

The continual drone of thunder and almost constant blasts of lightning had lulled most to sleep, but many were restless and tossed in their blankets as the noise of the night was thought to be nothing but an aggravation. The horse herd was separated from the village by the curve of the shore of the nearby lake and was watched over by the young warriors in training of the village. Those same young men sought shelter from the growing wind behind a cluster of close growing pines. The herd was restless, and the young men mounted their horses to ride around the herd and still the animals with their presence. The outlet of the lake was shown by the deeply carved ravine with the fast running stream in the bottom. With the noise of the stream, the lightning and thunder and the milling animals, the young men were oblivious to the danger that stalked their village.

The advancing flames now straddled both ridges that were the last barriers before the village. The lower swales between the ridges caused a natural chimney that drew the flames upward and toward the cluster of lodges. The sky was now illumined with the orange glow of fire and that same phosphorescence now stirred some of the Arapaho from their restless slumber. The roar of the fire overpowered the noise of the storm and several staggered from their lodges to momentarily stand transfixed at the approaching monster.

The cry was sounded and the village was soon filled with milling people seeking an escape from the overwhelming cloud of smoke that now obscured any indications of a way of escape. The turmoil and confusion took its toll as the conflagration began to lick at the outer perimeter of lodges. Screams and children's cries punctuated the lulls of the roaring inferno. The barked orders of men attempting to save the people were drowned out with the explosions of the sap laden pines. Finally, the milling crowd seemed to gain a semblance of order as they poured in the direction of the Northeast trail away from the flames.

The scream of an escaping cougar rolled Jeremiah from his covers causing him to run for the door, grabbing his Hawken that stood alongside it. Shield had exited in front of White Wolf and carried his rifle before him. Rushing to the corral expecting to see the animals under attack, their quick survey of the area revealed the animals were still frightened but from another cause. The horses lined the pole fence with ears pointing in the same direction and both men turned to see the cause for alarm. The orange luminosity that filled the arc of blackness over them rivaled the brilliance of a sunrise, but it was too early and not in the East. There was no mistaking the impending danger that threatened. Without delay, Shield began to rig the animals with the necessary tack while Jeremiah returned to the cabin to get Waters and Caleb. Within brief moments the four were mounted and riding the opposite direction from the flames. All were thinking about the village and the many family and friends now in the path of the all-consuming monster of wildfire.

Their exit trail dropped them from the thicker timber and nearer the edge of the valley below. Riding farther into the flats, they stopped at the edge of a stream and turned to view the path of the fire. It was a broad brush of destruction that painted the mountainside with the blackness of death. The grey light of early morn lifted the curtain of uncertainty to reveal a black path across the formerly blue mountainside. From the valley to timberline nothing remained for almost five miles. The leading edge of the fire was sputtering at the border of several parks on the higher ridges of the mountain, and stubborn flames still licked at the scattered trees.

As they looked back at the mountainside, all could see where the village had been. Although protected in many ways by the contour of the land and the surrounding trees, that protection had turned on them and what little could be seen from below was destroyed.

"We must go back. There may be those that are hurt and need help. We must go," stated Waters emphatically.

"You ain't gettin' any argument from me, girl. The horses are watered and the fire is down so it's back we go," agreed Jeremiah.

As the four entered the clearing to find the cabin intact and knowing the fire had passed them by, they looked to see several from the village stumbling down the trail towards their home. Led by Black Kettle, the stragglers revealed a number of injuries and burns on child and adult alike. Little conversation was heard as they filed into the clearing with many dropping on the scattered patches of grass for some relief and rest. The four dismounted and Caleb led the animals to the corral and began to strip the tack from each one.

Waters went to the cabin for blankets and bandages. Jeremiah and Shield began to assist the injured to a more comfortable place of rest in the shade of the cabin or the nearby trees. It was an overwhelming task facing the four and the few survivors of the fire that were uninjured.

WATERS TOOK THE SITUATION WELL IN HAND AS SHE escorted the more seriously injured into their cabin. Blankets had been spread in every available space as the furniture had been pushed aside. Waters had often assisted her father, Black Kettle, in the many ministrations of the office of Shaman or medicine man by gathering the many plants and herbs used in his work and occasionally she applied those remedies herself.

Now. digging into her meager supplies, she looked to her father with a question as to his supply. She knew she would soon have to make a foraging run throughout the area to replenish the needed plants. Black Kettle busied himself at the side of many of those severely injured, tending to the burn victims first. They had prepared poultices with crushed cat-tail roots, chickweed, and root of fireweed. With the soothing and cooling ointment applied, they overlaid it with leaves from the Hound's Tongue plant. With a light wrap to keep the poultice in place, the patients seemed to be relieved. Several remained in the cabin, while others more restless for the outdoors would leave the makeshift hospital.

Waters walked outside amongst the many gathered in small groups or near makeshift shelters and sought to aid any of the lesser injured. Some had minor cuts and scrapes received in their hasty retreat through the smoke-filled woods and Waters treated them with an ointment of the juice of berries of the Twisted Stalk plant. It was a cool and antiseptic ointment familiar to most woodsmen.

As she moved through her people, she noticed the elders had gathered in the shade of the nearby ponderosa and were seated in a circle on their individual blankets. It appeared they were engaged in a very animated discussion with arms waving and motions made as many looked out over the scattered people.

Everyone was concerned about their future, with the drought driving game away and now the fire... no one would be prepared to face a hard winter and many would probably die or starve. It was not a pleasant thought to consider the trial ahead for the entire village and the burden weighed heavy on the leaders. They must decide where the village would go and what preparations must be made. It would not be an easy decision and Waters knew her family would be very involved in whatever the council decided.

The restless night passed with few sleeping soundly. The fear that remained after the previous night's nightmare would not soon leave the minds and spirits of the many victims. Several had erected shelters in the clearing with the nearby brush and limbs from the many trees while others took shelter in the cavern and many chose to sleep in the open. Jeremiah and Broken Shield rose early in anticipation of the needed trip to the remains of the village to salvage whatever could still be used.

The council had chosen several of the other men to join the venture. During the night, the scattered herd of horses had been pushed to a larger meadow below the clearing by the young warriors that guarded the herd before the fire. It had been a tiresome task, but with the great need for the herd, the young warriors had proven their mettle. They had spent a long night gathering the scattered horses, but when they learned of the return trip to the village, every one of them volunteered for the task.

Relieved from their duties by other young men from the village, the four tired but re-energized men selected their own mounts and four additional horses to be used to pack any salvage. With Jeremiah and Shield and the other chosen men, the group now numbered ten men and nine additional pack horses, plus Jeremiah's two mules.

The sight that greeted the returnees was considerably different than the one they left. It was evident the many women had been busy. The brush shelters were made sturdy, as the Arapaho had often been called the "Brush Hut" people and only in recent seasons had adopted the hide teepees of the other plains Indians, and were well experienced at making strong shelters from nothing but brush and branches.

Several women were busy working the buffalo hides the men recently brought from their hunt and a large central cooking ring was cluttered with many strips of meat and roasts turning on green spits of willow.

Everyone was busy and the village resembled its former place full of active women and children.

When the men approached the clearing, the greetings were filled with questions as to the condition of the salvaged lodges and other goods. Families gathered together and unpacked the horses and the travois' that carried several lodges. The usually dark skinned warriors now appeared even more so and the entire group soon made their way below the clearing to the usual placid pool used by Jeremiah's family for bathing. The water soon ran almost as black as the soot that marked the many men but the refreshing dip raised the spirits of the entire group.

As the men straggled back into the clearing they made their way to the different family groups to help put things back together. When the council members saw Shield they motioned him to join them. After a brief conference, Shield turned to make his way to find Jeremiah. With little effort he located his friend in the doorway of his cabin as he leaned in searching for Laughing Waters. When Jeremiah turned from the door, Shield confronted him.

"The council has asked us to scout for another location for our village," he stated flatly. When the council gave a task to be done, it was never questioned for it was always considered a great honor to be given the task.

"And just where are we supposed to look for this new home for the village?" responded the young mountain man.

"Beyond the drought, maybe as far as the Absaroka."

"Ain't that Crow country?" inquired Jeremiah.

"Our people must have meat and shelter. There is none here so we must go far- but time is short. We must do whatever we have to do. Our people depend on us," came the sober response from Shield. Jeremiah was amazed at the strength of his friend. Shield's father, Tall Lance and his mother, Red Deer, had both perished in the fire as had seventeen others. It had been a somber salvage trip that revealed the devastation, but the need of the surviving members of the village had driven the men to complete the task and to put behind them the considerable loss.

Shield had been given a responsibility that would be difficult at best and oppressive under normal circumstances but now this burdensome assignment would give him a new focus that could possibly be helpful during his time of grief.

"So, who all's goin' on this scout?" sought Jeremiah.

"You, me, and the one who Talks with the Wind, if you want."

Jeremiah looked up with a sidelong stare at his friend, and asked, "You sure 'bout that? Don't they want others along on this shindig?"

"The others will be needed to hunt and provide for the village. There will be much to be done to prepare for the move."

"Well, it's a good thing we got those buffalo when we did. With what meat we already have in the cave yonder, I don't think anybody's goin' ta starve before we get back. I guess we're leavin' in the mornin'?" he surmised. Receiving a nod in the affirmative, Jeremiah stepped out to find his wife and break the news to her and Caleb.

Black Kettle had told his son-in-law that Waters had taken Caleb with her to hunt for more of the healing plants needed to tend to the many injured of the village. Jeremiah knew Waters favorite gathering places from the several times she wandered the trails while they were building their cabin. He headed to the streambed below the clearing to begin his search for his family and soon found them returning with bags full of greenery.

Caleb was doing his best to handle the two bags as he carried one and dragged the other. Waters had a good harvest and the smile that spread across her face said she was glad to see Jeremiah so he could help with the packing. On the winding pathway back to the clearing, the two discussed the coming trip that had fallen on the shoulders of her man and son.

"The last time I let you leave without me, you came back with a son," she smiled. "Do you plan on doing that again?"

With a chuckle as he put his free arm around her waist, he said, "The only young'un I expect to see soon is the one you're carryin'."

There were preparations to be made and the few remaining hours of daylight were well used. The men thoroughly checked their horses, tack, and other gear. Cleaning of their weapons would wait until after dark and done by the light of the lanterns in the cabin. Waters had a good stew that had simmered over the coals most of the day prepared for the evening meal and was enjoyed by all three men. Their parfleches were well packed with jerky, pemmican, and dried fruits and berries, as well as extra powder and shot.

No one knew how long the trip would take or how far they would have to go and they prepared as best they could. Taking only one pack animal, the paint mule, they would need to travel as fast and as far as possible in the short time allotted. In these mountains, winter could come early and hard.

The mountains of the Wind River Range were much like the other ranges of the Rocky Mountains. The tall mountains stretched their granite peaks heavenward and reached above the line where timber grew. From the timberline down, the skirts of pine that spread below the towering peaks stretched out on less steep ridged foothills that bore scattered treeless parks on one side of a ridge and the opposite side with a solid cover of the blue appearing spruce, pine and fir. The scouting party would travel in this shoulder area of the range between the foothills and the steeper stretches of the mountains. With an early start, Shield, Jeremiah and Talks with the Wind were well on their way as their backs were warmed with the spreading pink light of the rising sun.

THE CLUSTER OF TREES AND BRUSH WAS TOO THICK for a trail. A few crooked Cottonwood trees stretched their gnarly limbs to the sunlight and sheltered the scattered clusters of aspen and thick brush of willow and kinnikinnick. Clancy Mae and her big black fur ball of a dog, Two Bits, cowered in the small haven of the brush. She watched the attack on the wagons and the brutality of the battle by the Crow warriors. Often turning her head away from the bloody scene, she couldn't help but return her eyes to the atrocity.

She watched as the warriors gathered around the wagon of her mother and she saw the discharge of the shotgun that dropped two warriors. Her eyes were transfixed as she watched her mother impaled with the thrown lance and as she dropped on her face to the ground. Clancy buried her face in the thick fur of Two Bits and muffled her cry as her tears wet the collar of the big dog. Repeatedly Two Bits would mutter a low growl but each time he received a "Shush now, we can't let 'em know we're here."

Clancy dropped to her haunches at the side of her dog and peered through the thick brush at the lowest point beneath the thick branches. With her face to the ground, she watched as the Crow mutilated the bodies and ransacked the possessions within the wagons. It seemed like hours, but was more like twenty minutes, before the warriors finally mounted up and, leading the horses with their fallen comrades, trailed their leader across the meadow and disappeared in the trees beyond.

Still Clancy waited, never letting go of Two Bits and repeatedly burying her face in his thick fur to wipe away tears and to muffle the screams that sought to escape her trembling body. Finally, exhausted from the day, the trauma, and the grief, she curled up with her faithful companion and slept. It was only in the presence of Two Bits that she found any security and escape from the horrific images that paraded before her closed eyes.

The early morning light slowly filtered through the thick copse of trees and brush and sought to bring wakefulness to the frail figure of a girl and the big dog. Two Bits had been awake for some time but remained still to allow his charge additional rest. He faithfully waited for her to rise and start the new day together. The sight of her best friend beside her brought a fleeting smile to the girl as she stretched and sat up.

The sudden remembrance of the previous day's events made her drop to her vantage point and peek out to survey the sight of the massacre. With no movement from anything, she sat back up and hugged Two Bits and

said, "Well boy, it looks like it's just you and me now. I'm
not sure what we're gonna do, but I think we better see if
we can find anything we can use to help us make it,
maybe some blankets or food or sumpin'."

Pushing her way through the thick brush to the slight
trail, she followed the path to the river side camp. Strewn
with many personal items snatched from the wagons, the
campsite resembled the aftermath of a storm. The bodies
of the Indians had been removed but the bloody remains
of the hopeful travelers marred the grisly scene. Turning
her head away from the crumpled body of her mother,
Clancy walked to the wagon to search for any helpful
tool, memento, clothing or something to make a shelter.

She continually talked to Two Bits in a desperate
effort to chase away the loneliness that dogged her every
thought. "Two Bits, I know the right thing to do would be
to try to bury the folks, but I remember Mr. Evans
stopped us from buryin' those folks back by the North
Platte and he said 'If we bury 'em, the Injuns'll know we
was here and come after us,' and I sure don't want them
injuns comin' back after you an' me!"

Retrieving a woolen blanket, her momma's sewing kit,
and a coat from their wagon, Clancy started for the other
wagons to continue her search. The pile of plunder at the
foot of the nearby cottonwood began to grow. She added
a pair of Junior's britches and his coat, a tinder box with
flint and steel and tinder, a Bowie knife and scabbard
hidden beneath the seat of the Walcott wagon next to a
four-barrel pepperbox pistol. The pile grew with the
addition of a coffee pot and a skillet, a piece of the canvas
from a wagon bonnet, her mother's shotgun and some

stashed powder and shot from the Evans wagon and two more blankets completed her plunder.

"Now, what're we gonna do with all this stuff? It's more'n I can carry an' I ain't got a pack for you Two Bits, and where are we gonna go anyway?" The girl plopped herself down on her pile of rummaged goods, placed her elbows on her knees and her fists beneath her chin to begin formulating a plan of survival.

———

The scouting party led by Broken Shield drove themselves to make as much distance as possible. The continual up and down of the terrain lying between the foot hills and the more rugged mountains of the Wind River Range was a tiring trail for the travelers. The many stream beds in the bottom of the arroyos and ravines were as often dry as they were muddy but few were still live streams with any flow of water that was sufficient for the tiring animals and weary travelers. Without any discussion, Shield took a game trail that led downhill and into the valley below.

As they approached the edge of the tree line, the scouts gathered by Shield and waited while he dismounted and moved to survey the open meadow below them. It was late in the afternoon and this was the first stop of their long trek. Stretching his legs with his toes deep in his stirrups and hands on his saddle horn, Caleb asked, "Ain't we ever gonna stop? I know my horse is thirsty and could use a bit to eat and I sure am too."

"We'll probly stretch a bit here 'n then we'll be able to

make better time down here in the flats. Course we'll still need ta stay close to the tree line, but we should be able to find graze and water soon. I know out yonder is the Wind River and I'm sure it's got water, but we can't just go runnin' out there. Ya never know what's waitin'," surmised Jeremiah.

Shield returned and mounted up to lead the way into the clearing of the valley. Jeremiah shrugged to his boy and received a similar expression in return. It was no more than a hundred yards along the tree line that a small tributary to the Wind River chuckled down the shallow ravine on its way to the bigger river. A small clearing just in the edge of the trees was the objective of the leader of the group and the trio quickly made do with what would certainly be a short rest stop.

Loosening the cinches on their mounts and the pack mule, the animals were taken to water and tethered to graze on the nearby grass at the edge of the stream. The men returned to the small clearing to stretch out and refresh themselves with a handful of pemmican and a long drink of water. In less than an hour, Shield was on his feet and ready to mount up and take to the trail again. Jeremiah commented, "You're movin' like you got some place in particular in mind. Whatcha thinkin'?"

"It will take maybe three days before we cross over to the Absaroka. I know a good valley up high in the timber that will make a good winter camp, but it is Crow country. If we travel here in the valley instead of up higher where we were, we will be able to see more sign of our enemy and know if they have been here. Too much sign, not good to make camp there and will look in other areas.

If we cannot camp, it will take too long to find other camp."

"Well, Shield, one thing I learned on that long trek with Scratch is that things always have a way of workin' out. I'm sure we'll be able to find a good place for your people and we can start layin' in winter supplies and it'll be all right," assured Jeremiah, then thought to himself, *I just wish I believed that my own, durn self.*

Late afternoon of the third day brought the craggy peaks of the Absaroka into a clear view off their right shoulder. Shield had ventured across the river and had crossed a several day old trail of wagons traveling through the valley that brought some consternation to the scouts but there was little sign of the Crow. Continuing on the trail on the west side of the Wind River the scouts were observant of several tracks of buffalo, elk, deer, antelope and bear but none in abundance. The occasional sighting of game only served to remind the scouts of the scarcity of meat animals in this time of drought.

As dusk approached, Shield said they would make camp near the river where a finger of Aspen reached toward the waterway. It was a well-protected area tucked into the trees and not visible from the open meadow that was chosen by Shield. As Jeremiah and Caleb watered their horses and began to remove saddles and packs, Shield signaled he would make a survey of the area and scout for any game or potential problems.

As dark descended on the small camp, the glow of the campfire was shielded by the thick grove of Aspen that rattled their leaves in protest to the invaders. The pan on the fire held smoked buffalo, fresh turnips and onions and a smattering of mysterious seasonings from Waters private stock. The water softened the meat and tendered the vegetables as the aroma of nature's stew caused stomachs to groan in anticipation.

Shield returned and squatted near the fire and spoke softly, "The wagons are upstream about a mile. It looks like the Crow caught them, maybe three or four days ago. I did not go close but I could see some bodies. No sign of life. We will look tomorrow."

It was a somber trio that left their camp the next morning before daybreak. The few remaining stars were tucking themselves behind the dark shadows of cloud to disappear for the coming dawn.

Three horses and one mule moved as quietly as possible along the dusty game trail just inside the tree line at the edge of the Wind River valley. It had long been the habit of these travelers to secure any loose tack items that might make a sound as they moved, unlike the usual careless traveler that was not used to the necessity of silence in the wilderness. With no conversation and only hand signals, the scouts neared the site of the remains of the wagons.

Shield moved further upstream before dropping through the scattered Aspen to the west side of the Wind River. Jeremiah and Caleb prepared to approach the river crossing near the site of the wagons as they checked the loads in their rifles and laid them across their legs behind the saddle horns. Jeremiah led out, trailed by his pack horse and with Caleb bringing up the rear. Both scouts were very observant for any movement that would betray a trap. They decided before the action they would take if surprised by anyone, but everything was still.

A few fat ravens, one hawk and one starving coyote that had been feeding on the rotting flesh and bleached bones, froze at the sight of the visitors. Within moments, the coyote turned tail and the movement startled the birds to flight. The presence of the different predators gave assurance to the two visitors that there were no other dangers nearby.

The stench of the carrion gave haste to Jeremiah as they rode through the debris of the three wagons and their former inhabitants. He noted a few broken shafts of arrows and a lance that told him the perpetrators were the Crow. Here was evidence of the enemy of the Arapaho that Shield had been looking for during their scout. They rode about forty yards from the remains and stopped in the shade of the tall cottonwoods by the stream. Jeremiah knew Shield would scout the nearby area and join them shortly. Stepping down from his mount, he asked Caleb if he wanted to stretch his legs.

"Sure. I was just thinkin' 'bout all those people. What were they doin' here and where were they goin'?"

"Like most folks, they were probably chasin' a dream. So many folks back East of here live in places like you and your family did, but they don't have a lot of room for farms and such, then along comes someone that tells about free land in Oregon territory and how beautiful it is and how rich the soil is and how everything is growin' and they even sometimes tell 'em there's gold and silver to be found.

So, folks get ta' dreamin' and thinkin' and the next thing ya know, they're on their way. But, they don't know how hard this country can be, and they don't know anything about survivin' in the wilderness with Indians an' all, but they can't give up the dream, so out they come. And here they die," stated Jeremiah.

"Guess I can't fault 'em none. I remember wanderin' the woods and dreamin' 'bout coming out West. But it seems a shame, here they be, buried with their dreams, and nobody's gonna know what happened or where they are, just bones by a river bank."

Jeremiah was a little surprised at the insight and compassion of his adopted son, but he was pleased that he thought of others as more than just another being, but someone with dreams and goals and hopes as well. He knew that when someone sees others with like feelings as their own, it is then that better understanding of one another yields greater harvests from which everyone benefits. His pensive thoughts were interrupted by the arrival of his friend and Jeremiah waited for Shield to share what his facial expression foretold.

"There is another, a young girl. She has made a camp farther upriver and it is well hidden. I crossed her trail and followed it to her camp. She is his age but not as big, has fire for hair and is good in the woods. There is a big black wolf, I think, with her. Bigger than any other wolf, maybe not a wolf but just a dog."

"She's all alone? How long do ya' figger?" asked Talks to the Wind.

Motioning to the remains of the wagons, Shield responded, "Since that happened, three or four days ago. She must have hidden in the trees or somewhere."

"Guess we better go see if we can help her then," surmised Jeremiah with a shrug and started to mount up.

"Oh-oh, I know where this is headed and Ma ain't gonna let you live it down. 'Member what she said when you left?" asked Caleb referring to the comment made when they parted. "She said the last time she let you go you came home with me and she asked if you were gonna bring home 'nother un' and you said no. Ha!"

Shield was leading the way to the girl's camp but stopped before approaching. "You go to the camp. She might be afraid if she sees me, she might think I am like those that attacked the wagons."

"Ya got a point there Shield. You keep the mule; me'n the boy'll see if we can approach her without scarin' her ta' death."

Nearing the small clearing, Jeremiah called out, "Hello the camp!" but received no answer. "Hello the camp! We're comin' in, we're friendly and mean no harm." With one hand raised high while the other held his Hawken and Caleb copying Jeremiah's example, the two rode slowly into the camp. It had been well concealed. She had used the canvas to make a shelter but was careful enough to cover it with branches to hide the dirty white of the wagon's bonnet. The small fire ring was beneath the overhanging branches of a large spruce that would shield the fire from view and disperse any smoke. Near to the stream for easy access but with enough tree cover on all sides to make the camp difficult to see, she had laid it out as well as any seasoned mountain man.

A threatening growl came from the thicker undergrowth by the tall Spruce but the men could not see its source. The click of hammers on a shotgun revealed the threatening moves of someone in the brush. "Who are you and whatta ya want?" came a voice that was obviously disguised to sound deeper.

"Young lady, my name is Jeremiah and this is my son, Caleb. Our friend followed your trail from the wagons and unless I miss my guess, you could use a friend. This is no country for anyone to be alone, so why don't you come on out and let's see if we can help each other, okay?"

They waited patiently while the girl was making up her mind. Caleb looked at Jeremiah and shrugged his shoulders with his palm out and up in the form of a question and received a shrug from Jeremiah with a scowl that said wait. Soon, a hand pushed aside the lower branch of the thick blue spruce and a mop-headed ragamuffin with freckles across her nose and packing a shotgun with both hands picked her way toward the visitors. Without a word she approached the two, walked slowly around behind them and back to the front of them and said, "What're you doin' out here anyway?" addressing herself to Caleb.

"We live in these mountains, that's what," answered the boy with a touch of irritation in his voice.

She looked to Jeremiah for affirmation of his answer and Jeremiah nodded his head. "That's right, I've lived in these mountains... well, south of here anyway, since I was your age. So, welcome to our home."

She visibly began to relax as she lowered the shotgun to stand it on its butt on the ground beside her. With a snap of her fingers, a monster of a black dog trotted from the trees to stand beside her with a stance that told of his protective manner. Dropping her hand to his head, she said, "I'm Clancy Mae and this is Two Bits. He's my best friend and protector." The dog tensed as he looked beyond the two visitors and growled a warning at the approach of Shield. Clancy reached for the shotgun but the warning from Jeremiah stayed her hand.

"Whoa, don't go shootin' him. That's Broken Shield and he's our friend. I grew up with him and he will not hurt you. He's the one that found your trail and your camp." Turning back to Shield, he said, "Shield, come meet Clancy Mae." At his approach, the girl fingered the shotgun but did not raise it. Jeremiah continued, "Shield is an Arapaho. Those that attacked your wagons were Crow and the enemy of the Arapaho. We are here to scout out a place to move their village. There was a big fire a few days back and several were lost and they need a new place with more game and a safe place to winter. Can we get down and continue this conversation over some coffee and maybe a little bit to eat?"

"I ain't got no coffee and I sure ain't got much to eat," stated Clancy emphatically.

"No, no. We have the coffee and food, it's just kinda hard to fix it while we're still on horseback," he said as he dismounted. Following his example, Caleb and Shield joined him and began to prepare for an early lunch break. Caleb took the coffee pot and coffee from the pack and walked toward the river for some water. Clancy seated herself on a log at the edge of the fire ring and watched as the men tethered the horses closer to the river and at the edge of the clearing by the grass.

After they ate and thoroughly discussed the situation with Clancy, all agreed the only sensible course was for her to join the scouts and then return to the village with them. Adding the parfleche and saddle bags from Caleb's mount to the pack mule, Clancy was to ride behind Caleb. At first Caleb was a little aggravated, but soon became comfortable with the company behind him.

By the end of the day, the travelers had reached the northwest end of the valley and the headwaters of the Wind River. It was here that Shield had told them they would turn to the northeast to the headwaters of the Shoshone River and cross it to the saddle and valley that Shield thought would be the next location for the village.

THE HIGH COUNTRY OF THE UPPER REACHES OF THE Wind River valley was a blend of Fir, Pine and scattered Aspen groves. The surrounding mountains formed a three-sided bowl with sides that slid down to the valley below. The many colors of greens and blues of the conifers were interspersed with the white bark of the Aspen and the grays and browns of the boulders and slide rock. The smattering of colors, shapes and contours formed a masterpiece of art from the Creator's hand.

In the basin of this natural bowl was cradled the group of scouts on a mission to find a new home. Three of the four still slumbered as the morning sun teased the day with colors from below the eastern horizon. Shield was on a walking scout of the surrounding area. The trail yielded no fresh sign of any other visitors to the valley, but with the remains of the wagons still fresh in his mind, caution was the standard for the coming day.

Their present location was contested territory. The head of this valley and the nearby mountain pass was at the apex of the territories of the Gros Ventre to the west, the Peigan Blackfoot to the north, the Arapaho from the south and the Crow to the east. At any time, any or even all of these peoples could have raiding or hunting parties that would meet- and conflict would inevitably be quick and deadly.

Yet Shield believed the area where they were headed was a valley that could be held by the Arapaho and would seldom see any of the neighboring tribes contest their presence. The nearest would be the Crow but their primary territory was on the east side of the Absaroka in the valley of the Bighorns and east to the Bighorn Mountains. There had been conflict between the two peoples in the past, but those times had not been frequent.

Usually when the Crow went on raiding parties they preferred to go to the southeast to Sioux territory or further south into Cheyenne country. When the Arapaho mounted a raid for horses or honor it was usually against the Shoshone or Ute and sometimes against the Gros Ventre. However, Shield knew if their presence was known, it could be contested by the Crow, but that would usually depend on how far their villages were into the Bighorn Valley as most would not mount a major raid that took them too many days away from their village and leave their own people exposed to others.

With no fresh sign for alarm, Shield returned to the camp as the others were rousting out and preparing the morning meal. The small, smokeless fire had Jeremiah's coffee pot at the side and a pan full of salt pork sizzling. The pork had been Clancy's contribution from her plundered stores from the wagons. It was the last of her rations but needed to be used before spoilage claimed it all. While the pork sizzled, Clancy whipped up a batch of Johnny cakes and prepared to replace the pork with the batter in the frying pan.

Caleb hadn't enjoyed the cornmeal staple since he left home in Michigan and was surprised to see the girl preparing the mix. Although Jeremiah and Waters had both used cornmeal and made a type of cake, it wasn't the same as Johnny cakes. Caleb watched as she added some sugar and motioned for her to add a bit more. With a smile, she complied as both the youngsters enjoyed the sweeter taste in the cakes.

He fondly remembered the times his mother had made them for him and they had drowned them with maple syrup. Unfortunately, the mountains of the Rockies were devoid of Maple trees, however, he hoped to get some honey the next time they were in the lower elevations where the honey bees swarmed.

With the morning meal finished and their gear packed, the scouting party started for the trail to the high mountain valley. The game trail followed the contour of the flanks of the mountain and stayed about twenty yards into the trees. It was easy going and they made good time. Crossing over one ridge brought them into an open park, but the trail held to the uphill side of the thick cover of scrub oak, sometimes called buck brush, that covered the lower portion of the large open park on the east side of the ridge. By staying near the brush, they could not be seen by anyone on a lower trail or in the valley below which was the practice of the trail making Wapiti or elk of the timberline areas of the mountains.

Shield pointed to a granite topped peak directly to the east and then turned to point at one over their left shoulder and North. These were the two highest mountains near them and Shield said, "The park we go to is between these mountains and across the next stream. It is a good valley and somewhat hidden and I think will be safe."

Jeremiah nodded as he surveyed the area, becoming familiar with all the evident landmarks and the differing terrain. Looking below them to the valley that spread out to the east and south, Jeremiah could see this was in the higher reaches of the area and would probably have considerable snowfall in the winter. Game was more plentiful and it was evident the snowmelt from the previous winter had maintained the greenery of the area. As long as they were able to lay in a goodly amount of meat, the winter could be tolerated. Now, if only they didn't have to fight anything but the elements to survive, this could be a good winter.

The trail continued easterly and dropped off the hip of the ridge now behind them, continuing for another couple of miles before turning back to the north. Late afternoon saw them crossing the headwaters of the Shoshone River and climbing the north bank where the valley opened before them.

Lining the river bank, the visitors to the valley surveyed the area before them. With the Shoshone River at this end and another small creek that Shield told them ran on north into a large lake, there would be ample water. The entire valley was carpeted with thick and tall grasses and the streams were lined with a plentiful supply of willows that were often used for hide frames, arrow shafts, drying racks and many other uses. The valley lay between two mountain ranges that could provide either shelter from severe winds but sometimes ramparts that held the snows.

However, the southerly facing hillside would be the location for the village and would catch the warm sun for most of the day. Shield looked to Jeremiah and was evidently looking for approval which White Wolf readily offered. "Yessir, I think you done good, Shield. I think this will be a fine place for the village. It looks like three different directions we can go for game." He gestured, "North there, didn't you say there's a lake farther down the valley? And it looks like this stream here," pointing to the retreating Shoshone, "cuts through those mountains and probably leads to good huntin' an,' of course, the valley we just came from. Yup, looks good to me," he said approvingly with a smile spreading through his whiskers.

With the mountain range to their west, the sun had already dropped below the peaks but dusk had not dropped her skirts. Following Shield to the edge of the trees to the east edge of the clearing and the potential site for the village, the scouts anticipated making camp for the night. It was good to know their scout was successful and they would start for home in the morning.

Their thoughts had not lingered on the people of the village, though their trek was for their benefit, but now with the mission complete their minds returned to their family and friends and the struggles they were enduring. When the scouts returned, they knew it would be a difficult move to return to this valley and some of those more critically injured might not survive the trip, but it was a necessary move for the survival of the people.

As they unpacked the gear from the mule and their mounts, the usual chores fell to each person. Caleb would collect the firewood, Jeremiah would prepare for the meal with Clancy assisting, and Shield would tend to the horses. Soon all were gathered near the small blossoming campfire and anxiously awaiting the evening meal. By the time dusk retreated and darkness enveloped the small campsite, all were ready to turn in for the night. Jeremiah and Shield would spell each other during the night so someone was on watch at all times. The night was clear, the stars filled the black sky and the gentle sounds of the night comforted the weary travelers.

———

The Eelalapito Crow band picked their way through the dense pine along the narrow trail. Nearing the end of their raiding excursion the previous day, they cut the trail of several horses moving toward the end of the valley. It was unusual to see others in this area unless they were from the Blackfeet or Gros Ventre. Normally it was too far north for the Arapaho but within the range of enemy raiding parties from the northern tribes.

Early on their raid, before they hit the small village of the Gros Ventre, they had struck the white man's wagons and taken several weapons and other plunder. They did not think this trail could be more white men from those wagons, they were certain they had killed all those that traveled in that group, but they worried. The advance scout was returning along the trail and approached Barcheeampe, Pine Leaf, their war leader.

Strikes Enemy stopped the scout with a nod of his head and motioned for him to speak to Pine Leaf with his report. Walks With a Limp was a good warrior and able scout and his report would be thorough and accurate. "They camped just past the Aspen and left early this morning. They took the trail through the trees and around the point," he motioned with his outstretched arm to the ridge below the granite peak to the East.

Leaf said, "The tracks show four animals, what does the camp say?"

"They wiped out most sign, covered it with pine needles and leaves, but all tracks but one are moccasins. There are three with moccasins, two large, one smaller. One with white man's shoes, small, woman."

"Moving fast or not?" asked the leader.

"No, but careful."

"White men, Gros Ventre, or can you tell?" quizzed Pine Leaf. Her blood vengeance for any white man drove her often beyond reason.

"Maybe Arapaho," answered Walks With a Limp.

"Arapaho? But with the white woman, maybe from the wagons," she pondered. "We will go further, but not try to strike until in the morning, if we catch them. We have more men and weapons... the fight will be easy."

Strikes Enemy took the lead as the ten warriors and their leader Pine Leaf followed on the winding path beyond the campsite that had been used by Jeremiah and company. Shield had back-tracked the scouts and thoroughly worked over the trail and their tracks in an attempt to elude any that might seek to follow them. Using a pine branch, Aspen leaves, dry needles from under a tall Ponderosa and loose dust from beside the trail, he made it appear as if nothing had followed the high trail but both elk tracks and horse tracks took the lower trail that dropped below the Scrub Oak.

Without close examination, Strikes Enemy led the party along the lower trail before looking for a camp spot. Dusk had fallen and darkness was draping the mountain valley when the war party moved from the trail to the small clearing within the pines. Camp would be made here and the pursuit of the invaders of the valley would resume with first light.

———

The natural lay of the land between the two opposing ranges of granite-topped mountains was a long saddle with marshes and seeps from the long lasting snow pack of the low valley. The trail through the valley and over the pass that would drop down to the Wind River was a long used trail of the many different tribal peoples.

A favorite route of raiding Blackfeet, they would first hit any villages of the Nez Perce to the north of the great lake, then go for the Gros Ventre in the valley west of the mountains and east of the Snake River, then over the pass to raid into the Crow country that lay to the east of this mountain range.

It was just such a raid that was led by Bear Killer from the Peigan band of the Blackfeet. Sixteen warriors chose to follow the proven leader when he boasted of the many scalps that covered his hide shield and hung in his lodge. Many young warriors anxious to prove themselves as warriors sought the chance to join him but he was selective of those he would take with him, as *proven* warriors had grown tired of hunting trips that brought no honor. Many were anxious to capture horses, scalps and even women to be taken as slaves or mates, but all wanted the honor of a raid with the respected and feared Bear Killer.

When they attacked the Gros Ventre, they were disappointed to learn the Crow had already taken any worthy plunder and only a few old men and women remained in the desecrated village. Angered that they were beaten to the prize by the Crow, Bear Killer determined to gain vengeance against the intruders to their raiding territory.

As the raiders followed their leader, his horse dropped from sight when the trail began its descent into the lower and more open valley of the Wind River. As the trail approached the tree line near the bottom of the descent, Bear Killer stopped and held up a hand for his followers to stop. He slipped from his mount and was joined by Plenty Coups, his most trusted companion.

As they examined the trail, they spoke animatedly with one another with both making many gestures both up and down the trail. The two leaders agreed the Crow had taken the trail and possibly were following some others before them. With the trail fresh, but with light dwindling, they agreed to make camp and track the Crow early. Bear Killer told Plenty Coups, "You follow and scout them, but also for a good ambush site. We will take them tomorrow and show them the price of entering our territory. They will all die and we will take many scalps."

With the trail so recent, Plenty Coups chose to follow the path on foot, leaving his mount with his fellow warriors and disappearing silently into the trees.

A FLAT-TOPPED BOULDER PROVIDED A SEAT FOR Jeremiah as he slipped from his bedroll just before the morning light of gray began to show. He knew he had much to be thankful for and he sought the solace of time with his God, knowing that those moments of greeting a new day in the company of his Lord and Savior gave more comfort and courage to meet the challenges of any new day before him.

The quiet reverie also heightened his senses to everything around him as he became more conscious of the Creator's hand in the wondrous world that held him in awe. The gentle breeze that dropped from the cool heights and down to the warmer basin of the valley would lift up into the sheltering pines above. Then, filtered through the outstretched needles of the grasping conifers, it would caress the upper valleys to bring the remaining sheltered snow into the streams as fresh water. But it was that gentle breeze that carried an alarming warning to the prayerful man on the boulder. He stood and lifted his head as if the added height would heighten his ability to detect the direction and source of the scent. He turned quickly and made for the camp.

"We've got company comin'," he said to Shield who was preparing to start the morning fire. Looking up to Jeremiah and noting the alarm on his face, he questioned with an outstretched hand, palm up.

"Bear Grease," was the only response needed. Both men knew it was a common practice for warriors to slick down their hair as part of their preparation for battle. Also used by women to aid their grooming, it was more commonly used by the warriors because of its recogniz- able odor. Many things were used by warriors to intimi- date their opponents, war paint, war cries, weapons, image and even the smell of bear grease or anything else that could strike fear into others. But it was the odor of bear grease worn by warriors that was carried by the breeze to the camp high above the trail that would soon be traveled by the Crow and unknown to either the Crow or Jeremiah, but worn by the Peigan Blackfeet.

The early morning light found the Crow well on the trail in pursuit of those they considered invaders to their territory. Pine Leaf was focused on the hunt for the white man and the one that escaped from the wagons, the possi- bility of an Arapaho would be an added coup for her band of raiders. But it was that focus of vengeance that blinded her to the threat that was looming before her band and presented a greater danger.

Walks With a Limp had scouted the trail ahead, but it was his oversight that caused them to take the lower trail they now traveled on, the trail that took them below the thick growth of scrub oak. They would wait until the prey was located before planning their attack. By Walks observation, he thought they should overtake the invaders by mid-day. If they followed this trail, though the path yielded little evidence of travel, they should come upon them soon and decide the best means of attack.

Always the cautious one, Walks With a Limp had dispatched two warriors to shadow the upper trail to ensure their prey had not eluded them with any subterfuge and were camped in a higher park. Walks was familiar with the area and knew of the upper park between the two higher peaks. Now the entire party was anticipating another opportunity for coups and scalps by whatever means and in whatever location necessary.

The Peigan Blackfeet leader, Bear Killer, was a veteran of many raiding parties and had always been victorious with a leadership that yielded many honors for those that fought alongside their leader. It was that experience that prompted his decision to take advantage of the moonlight of the clear night and prepare the trap for the Crow band that was the target of his hunt.

Each time he thought of the strike by the Crow on the Gros Ventre village he had planned to target, that resulted in an embarrassment for him and his raiders, anger seethed within him. He had never been bested in any way by an enemy and he would not allow this to be a mark on his record of honors, now.

The late night scout by Plenty Coups revealed the number of the Crow and now Bear Killer was assured the greater number of the Blackfeet and the element of surprise guaranteed him a victory over their hated enemy.

To strike them in their own territory would be an added honor and satisfaction. Plenty Coups had taken two warriors with him on the scout during the night, and they had traveled the lower trail to give the Crow the impression their quarry had taken that path toward the furthermost ridge with the many fingers of pine that provided an ideal location for an attack.

Three young Blackfeet warriors were given the task of taking the horses beyond the next ridge to the bottom of a bald park with a small stream. They were to keep the animals quiet and out of sight of the proposed location of attack. Although not directly involved in the coming battle, they were reminded of the importance of protecting the animals, a task they begrudgingly undertook but, never the less, realized the need. If they proved worthy of this, perhaps they would have the opportunity to be directly involved in the next battle. The remaining fourteen warriors were busily taking their places for the coming conflict.

Bear Killer was thorough in assigning places for each of the fighters. The trail led through a level area that was somewhat clear of trees and shrubbery but provided many outcroppings of rock and fallen timber on the slope that rose away from the clearing. The path that led to the opening was narrow as it wound through the thick trees before opening to the clearing. This would require the Crow party to enter single file and by the time they entered the park, they would be spread out and would be vulnerable targets.

The downhill side of the clearing offered a tempting opening for escape, but if taken, would lead to a secondary attack. Of those awaiting attackers, most were armed with bows and arrows or lances, but a few had muskets. Those with muskets would be at the far side of the attack area and would be the barrier to turn any fleeing Crow to take the downhill escape route. Within an hour after the break of dawn, the attackers were in place and prepared for the coming conflict.

Shield motioned for Jeremiah to follow him as he trotted to the trees behind the camp. The path he followed led the two men to a high outcropping of granite that was an excellent promontory that overlooked the entire valley and hillsides below. Dropping to their bellies before approaching the edge, the two carefully surveyed the entire area that lay before them.

Knowing their peripheral vision would likely reveal any movement, they slowly scanned the scattered clearings, pathways, and exposed parks. The movement on the ridge to their left caught their eyes and both grunted as they watched the three young warriors taking the horses over the next ridge. Carefully examining the back trail of the horses, the edge of the small clearing just inside the tree-line was marked by the movement of warriors taking up positions for an attack. While Shield continued his observation of the Blackfeet, Jeremiah brought his gaze across the terrain below them and back toward the tree-line along the more northern ridge. Movement. The approaching Crow exited the tree line at a good walking pace watching the trail before them as if they were on the track of something or someone. Their casual manner and carriage revealed their lack of fear of attack, but more of an anticipation of being the attackers. Jeremiah realized the Crow had no idea of what awaited ahead on the trail they traveled.

"Well, at least I don't think we're the object of their hunt," observed Jeremiah.

"I wiped out our trail at the junction of the two trails at the edge of the trees, we took the high trail and the one they follow leads below the oak. Maybe they are after us, but don't know about the Blackfeet," surmised Shield.

"So, do we get involved, or should we use this opportunity to make our getaway?"

"Both the Crow and the Blackfeet are our enemies. But we want to live here near the Crow and if we help them, maybe we can live without conflict for the coming winter," said Shield, thinking out loud but not with a great deal of conviction.

"Or we could get right in the middle of that coming fight, get ourselves killed and our families would not survive the winter," suggested Jeremiah.

"Yes, there is much at risk no matter what we do," stated Shield as he crawled back from the overlook, stood and turned to go back to their camp.

As they trotted down the trail, both men analyzed the choices confronting them and the many risks for them and the village. When they reached the camp, a look at one another answered both of their questions. When Caleb asked them what was up, Jeremiah began to instruct both Caleb and Clancy Mae as to what would be expected of them in the coming hours.

JEREMIAH KNEW THE HATRED THAT SHIELD harbored against the Blackfeet. He could not remember anyone, white or Indian, that held anything but hatred for them. Their reputation as vicious fighters and mutilators of their enemies was known throughout the mountains. With their home territory farther to the north, most would avoid going north of the Missouri River.

Often some arrogant trapper would boast of his willingness to confront "Bug's Boys" as some whites called them referring to sons of the devil, but if he carried through on his boast he would never be heard from again. The brutality of their attacks preceded them and the invoked fear served them well in battle. For Shield to choose to aid the Crow was testimony to his hatred for the Blackfeet. Jeremiah had fought the Crow before, but never the Blackfeet, and he wasn't looking forward to this set-to.

They returned to their promontory to plan their strategy and points of attack. They were able to observe the progress of the Crow and could anticipate when they would reach the projected point of attack. Carefully watching the clearing, there was no movement that would give away any presence, but their overlook enabled them to spot some Blackfeet below the clearing and speculate on their plan of a secondary attack.

Backing away from the edge of the outcropping of granite, they conferred with one another and determined the route and action each would take. Both would take their rifles and bows, while Jeremiah was also armed with his Paterson Colt pistol. The thick scrub oak provided good cover, but it was also thick enough to impede their progress with each step requiring careful movement of the branches and careful placement of their moccasins to prevent broken twigs and crushed leaves.

Jeremiah had farther to go to reach the lower shoulder of the mountain that would provide a field of fire for the secondary attack and he also had to cross the trail before the Crow. Shield readily made his determined place of shelter but Jeremiah's route proved more difficult.

Nearing the edge of the buck brush, Jeremiah dropped to his belly to view the trail before emerging from his cover. With a straight line view of the game trail, he saw the legs of an approaching horse. Slowly backing further into the brush but keeping his line of sight, he watched as the war party of the Crow filed along the trail with each horse's nose within inches of the tail of the one before. There was something different about the second rider, enough so that Jeremiah slowly lifted his head to see through the brush and define what he thought he saw.

He was right, that one was a woman, but she was attired and armed like the rest of the warriors. The many feathers intertwined in the braids that trailed down her back told of her rank and if Jeremiah was correct in what he was thinking, this was the war leader of the pack. He slowly dropped back to his stomach and waited, thinking about the woman as a leader.

He had heard of a war leader named Pine Leaf that was known for her brutality and that her ferocity equaled the reputation of the Blackfeet. *This is going to be quite a battle*, thought Jeremiah. Within moments of the last warrior passing, Jeremiah slipped from his cover to cross the trail and make his way through the scattered pines and brush to his chosen point for his role in the coming conflict.

The Blackfeet had been in position and still for long enough for the birds to return. A squirrel scolded a camp-robber Jay for coming too close to his nest in the gray dead snag of an old pine. The chirp of a bright yellow mountain canary trilled through the towering pines. But as the Crow war party approached, the black-topped Jay sounded the alarm. Just the presence of the bird put the Crow at ease, knowing if there had been any recent activity the birds would have flown before they arrived.

Strikes Enemy rode in the lead aboard his favorite war pony, a long legged all black stud that had served him well in many fights, yet the Blackfeet were so well hidden and so still, even the horse was not alarmed. The column of Crow cautiously began entering the pine surrounded clearing.

Shield had taken his position above the entrenched

Blackfeet, yet within easy bowshot. Those lurking below had camouflaged themselves well, but were focused on those to their front and had little thought or expectation of any danger from above them. As they waited, Shield examined each one to see if he could determine which one was the leader. Knowing the leader would position himself at a point with a good view of the conflict, Shield rightly assumed the leader would be on the uphill side of the attack.

Almost in the center of the six warriors hidden behind the rocks and downed timber, knelt one with several feathers held in a cluster at the back of his head. He was tall, muscular and confident. With hand signals, he directed his men to ready themselves. Shield's overview of the clearing and nearby timber revealed to him the position of the other warriors that were obscured in the timber alongside the trail that exited the clearing. Knowing there were others below the clearing, Shield knew what the plan was and prepared himself. He would wait until the attack began, then when the rifles to his left began to fire, he would try to take out the leader with his rifle. If he revealed his position too soon, he would endanger himself and not accomplish his chosen task.

As the Crow neared the clearing, the trees on the downhill side provided enough cover for Jeremiah to locate a good vantage point and clear field of fire. He stealthily made his way to a cluster of ponderosa on a slight knoll that would overlook the escape route from the clearing. He surveyed the area quickly to find the stationed Blackfeet who had prepared themselves for the secondary attack. As discussed with Shield, he looked for one that would be the apparent leader of this group and spotted a warrior with a top-knot of hair held in place with a band of beads that also trailed feathers down his back. He was on the opposite side of the apparent trail and partially obscured by some stunted Aspen. He would be Jeremiah's primary target.

With Strikes Enemy in the lead, the column entered the clearing. Pine Leaf spoke to Strikes to wait and he moved his mount to the side of the trail to enable Pine Leaf to move beside him. The column continued to enter the clearing and crowded together awaiting their leaders to continue. Pine said, "We should have seen more sign. How far ahead are they?"

"We should be nearing them when we near the ridge before us. They probably camped on the other side and we may catch them before. . ." The arrow that whispered through the shadows and pierced his throat cut his comment short. The impact caused him to reach to his neck as he toppled from his mount. Pine Leaf was not looking at him when he spoke and the sudden choking sound brought her attention immediately to her companion.

Immediately she dropped to the neck of her horse and kicked him to action, but as she neared the edge of the trees, muskets blasted with a thunderous roar and a blue cloud of smoke that spooked the horses.

When the first bowstring sang its death song, the others released their couriers of blood. The flight of arrows whispered in harmony as they sped to their intended targets. Most scored hits as the targets had not moved in alarm, but were still waiting on the leaders to continue on their trek. The air was filled with the cries of the wounded, the panicked screams of the horses, the angry war cries of the attackers and the shouted commands from the leaders.

Horses were rearing and pawing at the air as their wounded riders clawed at the reins or neck-ropes in their futile efforts to remain aboard. When the fusillade of fire from the muskets blocked the trail forward, those that remained mounted turned in their search for an escape route and pointed their horses to the break in the trees at the downhill side of the clearing.

Few of the Crow were able to return fire with their bows and the few rifles held by them. With the uncontrolled mounts and the smoke from the Blackfeet muskets they did not have time or target or ability to return fire. Five warriors lay with arrows protruding and eyes staring into emptiness, two others lay on the necks of their mounts with arms wrapped around the horse's necks in an attempt to make an escape. With a shrill scream and a cry, Walks With a Limp signaled his men to follow him on the downhill escape route.

When the attack began, Shield let fly his own arrows into the attacking Blackfeet. He dropped the one to his far right that was nearest the entry to the clearing. Then with another shot, he impaled the warrior next to the first. Stepping behind a larger boulder, he raised his rifle and almost simultaneously with the many muskets that blocked the Crow escape, he discharged his rifle and watched as the forehead of Bear Killer exploded in a shower of red. Stepping back behind the boulder, he immediately reloaded the rifle and set it aside.

Retrieving his bow, he searched for another target. The action in the clearing, the noise of the attack, and the position of Shield combined for an ideal disposition of death, and Shield willingly disposed of the vile enemy before him.

Three more were dealt death blows before the remaining warrior realized his companions had fallen. Standing and looking, he spotted Shield and drew back his bowstring with a nocked arrow to retaliate, but he was too slow and hesitant as the messenger from Shield delivered his notice of death as it was impaled deep in his left chest. He released his arrow to see it break upon impact with the stone before him and as blood bubbled over his chin, he looked at the feathers on the end of the arrow in his chest. Dropping to his knees, he grabbed at the arrow, looked to Shield, and fell on his face driving the arrow deeper into his lifeless body.

Pine Leaf's mount absorbed the musket ball intended for her and she rode her mount to the ground. With her bow beneath the fallen horse, she drew her tomahawk and charged the musket-armed warriors knowing she had a few moments before they could reload. With a piercing scream she launched herself between the branches that shielded the attackers and sunk her blade into the forehead of the nearest Blackfeet warrior.

As he fell she placed her foot on his chest and jerked her steel-bladed hawk from his skull and turned toward another. She was surprised by an explosion that knocked her backwards with an impact to her upper chest and enveloped her with a cloud of blue smoke. She felt herself falling backwards into a large spreading juniper bush.

Blackness covered her eyes and her last sight was of the overarching green branches of the evergreen brush.

The remaining Blackfeet that made up the force with muskets had successfully turned the charging Crow and now emerged from the shelter of the trees. They had been instructed to follow the retreating Crow but several turned aside to scalp the downed warriors in the clearing. When the first one drew his knife from his belt and bent to take the scalp, an arrow took him in the side, just below his armpit. With a strangled cry, he fell across the body of his intended target.

Two others had turned to the task of taking scalps and when the first took an arrow, they turned to locate the source of the attack. No sooner had they turned than two quickly launched arrows found their marks. One was taken just below the rib cage, while the other had his thigh pierced. Dropping to his side and grabbing the arrow in his leg, the second warrior tried to crawl to a place of cover behind a downed horse. Another attacker had turned back from the escape trail to see his fellow warrior crawling with his wounded leg.

Looking for the expected Crow, he stepped closer into the grassy area now littered with bodies. Within two steps of his friend, he felt the sudden impact to his chest and heard the discharge of the big rifle at the same time he saw the blossom of smoke by the boulder on the hillside. He dropped dead with his face splashing the pool of blood beside his childhood companion.

Hearing the attack commence on the hillside above them, Plenty Coups stepped from the cluster of Aspen and motioned his men to ready themselves. Within moments the noise of the battle increased with the blast of the fusillade from the muskets and the screams of the combatants. Shortly the trees parted as the Crow sought to escape down the narrow trail through the thick brush and trees. As Plenty Coups raised his arm to signal his men, Jeremiah squeezed off his shot and watched Plenty Coup's head snap back as the bullet took him just below his chin. Even from the distance, Jeremiah saw the red blossom on the man's throat as the Blackfeet leader was knocked back into the stunted aspen. Unknown to Jeremiah, as Plenty Coups fell, he was impaled on a jagged edge of a stump of a dead aspen, the grey wood thoroughly stained blood red.

The blast from Jeremiah's Hawken startled the Blackfeet and delayed their attack by seconds, but that brief delay allowed the Crow to give some retaliatory fire with both bows and lances. The resulting close fighting was evenly matched with each giving as much as they were getting, but the balance was turned in the favor of the few Crow by the repeated fire from Jeremiah.

First with his Hawken, and then his bow, he dealt the Blackfeet a hand of death as he dropped two more with his Hawken and as they turned on him, two that were running through the brush to attack him were stopped with his Paterson Colt. Then picking up his bow, he dispatched another with an arrow through the heart. The breaking of branches across the small ravine told of someone making their escape. Jeremiah could not see enough to take a shot and thought there might even be two that disappeared over the far ridge.

Silence commanded the site of the battle. Jeremiah

slowly walked toward the trail and the downed warriors that were sprawled on either side and into the brush. Blood colored the green of the juniper and kinnikinnick. He noticed the contrast of a small cluster of blue columbine that was untouched and added a splash of brightness to the canvas of death. Using the barrel of his Hawken to nudge each body for life, he held his Colt in his right hand at the ready. Most had bled out and were lifeless, one moaned but when Jeremiah kicked his body over, his guts spilled out of his opened belly and rolled to the downhill side.

The stench of death hung as if held down by the overarching branches of the pines and fir that surrounded the gruesome place of the end of dreams. Making his way uphill to meet Shield, Jeremiah was startled by the discharge of a musket. Knowing it was the sound of a musket and not of Shield's rifle, he quickened his step as he holstered his pistol and gripped his Hawken with both hands. Dodging from tree to tree, he made his way to the clearing and searched for Shield. His friend was leaning against a tree on the far side of the clearing with his hand held to his shoulder. Jeremiah quickly went to his side asking him what happened.

"There was one left hidden in the trees, I didn't see him until he fired. Go get my tomahawk from his back, over there," he implored as he motioned with his head to the trail into the trees. As Jeremiah started to the trail, Shield added, "I don't think there are any more, but look closely."

Within a few steps, it was evident that all the warriors were either dead or had fled. As he turned, Jeremiah heard a slight moan to his right and slightly down-hill in the brush. He cautiously stepped beside one tree, then another, once again hearing the moan. It was coming from deep in the juniper brush between the trees and in a shallow ravine. Probing with the barrel of his Hawken, he touched something that gave way with the feel of flesh. Pushing the branches aside, he saw the prostrate form of the woman warrior he saw earlier, *Pine Leaf! Now how am I gonna get you outta there, what with Shield havin' a bullet in his shoulder an' all.*

Jeremiah returned to the side of his friend and shared the news of the only survivor of the Crow being their war leader, Pine Leaf. Shield was startled not only at the news of a survivor, but that it was the woman with such a notorious reputation as a hater of whites and pretty much a hater of men. *Now what?* thought Shield as he looked at Jeremiah knowing his friend had the same question on his mind.

A WISPY FOG LAY LOW ALONG THE SHOSHONE CREEK at the bottom of the high mountain valley as the gentle breeze of the morning tugged at its feathery traces to rid the mountains of its mist. The trill of a meadowlark perched on a skeletal branch of dying pine drew Caleb's attention to its yellow breast. The cheerful melody of the beautiful bird always brought a smile to his face, for this was one of the more challenging bird songs for him to imitate. But his mimicry sounded as much like the original that most would think it but an echo.

Clancy Mae caught him in the act and expressed her surprise at his expertise. The two youngsters had been sequestered in a slight gulley protected by a long-ago uprooted large pine whose root ball provided a natural barrier to any curious searcher. A cluster of smaller pines and saplings gave additional cover for the young pioneers, both of whom were very well armed. Caleb cradled his Hawken across his chest and Clancy Mae's shotgun leaned against her side as she sought a comfortable position against the bank of the dry stream bed. While they huddled in the small depression, the horses had been tethered higher up in the trees in a small park with tall grass and a spring.

"So, is that the only bird-call you can do, or are there more?" inquired Clancy.

"Oh, I can pretty well do just about any of 'em, that's why Black Kettle gave me the name Talks to the Wind."

"Hmm, that was pretty good. Practice a lot, do ya?"

That was Caleb's cue to share his story with the redheaded girl. He began with his boyhood in rural Michigan, his life with his doctor father and his stepmother, and how Jeremiah came into his life.

"I always spent time in the woods when I was younger, but I only learned what I figgered out by myself. But when Jeremiah came, he's my mother's brother... my uncle, and I came West with him and Scratch, they schooled me on the ways of the wilderness and they say I 'took to it like a injun'. Course, when I lived with Jeremiah and Laughing Waters, and I spent my time with the kids of the village, I learned a lot from them," he boasted.

"You mean you lived with the Indians?" Clancy asked incredulously.

"Sure, my Ma... well, Jeremiah's wife, she's an Arapaho and my Pa, Jeremiah, he's an adopted member of the Arapaho and now I am too," he stated proudly.

Clancy just looked at him and shook her head in disbelief. She had never heard of a white boy living with the Indians. She thought all Indians wanted to kill all white people, like they did her Mom and Dad and all the others on the wagon train. The few days she had been with Caleb and Jeremiah, just being that close to Shield still scared her, but she had to admit to herself that he wasn't like she expected.

She knew there were different tribes and they had different ways, but she remembered most of the men on the wagon train thought all "redskins" were heathens and bad and should be killed. It had always bothered her because her Mom had always taught that Jesus said we should love one another, but most twisted that idea to mean just others 'like themselves'.

"So, tell me about yourself, Clancy- where were you from and where were you goin'?"

"We were from Ireland, although I don't remember anything about that or the voyage over here on the ship as I was but a wee lass at the time. Me father worked buildin' the Erie canal an' when he heard about the promised land in Oregon he said it sounded like home and thought we oughta go. So we packed up, bought a wagon and some horses, joined a wagon train and headed West.

It was a big wagon train, lots of wagons an' people, but some o' those me Pa was friends wid' were gittin' anxious and an ol' trapper tol' 'em 'bout a shorter route over the mountains and said they'd beat everybody else there and git the best land. So Mum and Pa talked about it an' we joined up wid' 'em and was comin' thru the valley there lookin' for Union Pass, some route found by Jim Bridger.

Then the Indians hit the wagons while I was in the brush. Me'n Two Bits usually wandered out in the brush lookin' for rabbits an' such." Clancy dropped her head to look at her hands in her lap as she remembered the attack. A tear wandered through her freckles to drop to her hands and she quickly raised her head and rubbed her eyes to dry her tears.

After a moment, Caleb quietly offered, "I lost my real Ma to sickness, an' then myPa married again and she was a real good Ma to me. But Pa died when he was tendin' a bunch o' folks that had the plague and then my new Ma died too. It sure hurts to lose your folks like that."

Clancy sniffed a little, wiped her nose and her eyes, and looked at Caleb realizing he *did* know how she felt. He reached out his hand for hers, she looked at it then up at him and placed her hand in his. This was a kinship formed in mutual loss and tragedy and strengthened by trial and commonality. They continued their conversation in low tones as each inquired of the other and reveled in the discoveries. Two Bits lay at the feet of Clancy and seemed to be in a fitful slumber as he would occasionally stir with a small whimper or snore. Clancy rested her feet on his thick fur and leaned back against the cool bank as the two escaped from the present situation with tales of childhood and dreams of the future.

Suddenly the two were startled by the distant sounds of battle. The rattle of gunfire sounded like far-off thunder that rolled through the timber in a staccato of terror. Both knew the sounds heralded the death of others and they hoped and prayed their friends would return unscathed. A few screams wafted through the timber, but the battle cries were faint and distant. The thought of the conflict caused Caleb to stretch up and peer over the bank, surveying the surrounding forest that sheltered them.

Jeremiah had said he was certain that no one would find them here and they would be safe, but he must still be vigilant because there are no guarantees when it comes to war parties, especially the Blackfeet. There was no observable movement within his eyesight and as he turned back to Clancy, he relaxed and settled back to his seat on the cool earth of the bank.

"Sounds like they're really mixin' it up down there, I'm sure Pa and Shield are givin' 'em fits though. They're two of the best fighters anywhere, 'cause that's what Black Kettle said. Cain't nobody whip my Pa."

"I hope they'll be all right. I'd hate to be up here without 'em," replied Clancy. She reached behind her to pull up a blanket around her shoulders. They were in the deep shade of the trees and sunlight would have a difficult time piercing the thick branches of the tall pines. The breeze that whispered through the lower reaches of the towering firs and pines came off the mountain tops still holding glaciers that shared their cold with the winds.

"It sure don't seem like it should be this cold this time of year. It must get really cold up here in the mountains come winter," observed Clancy.

"Yeah, it does, but it's not bad. You get used to it. Most just stay in their lodges and do stuff, like makin' arrows, or beadin' things, or making clothes and such," idly commented Caleb.

Two Bits raised his head, muttered a low growl and rose to look over the bank. He padded away at a trot and disappeared into the trees. Clancy turned to watch him go and whispered to him, but the dog didn't slacken his pace. Caleb gripped his Hawken and rose to look for the cause of the dog's alarm. He began to scan the downhill slope, peering through the trees as best he could. Bobbing his head and twisting to improve his view he searched for any movement. Looking for shadows, differences in color, listening for any sounds, he saw nothing to alarm him.

Continuing his visual search, he turned to scan to the side, and then to the rear and uphill from their small haven. Wherever his eyes went, the barrel of his rifle pointed. It was a common means of ensuring that every area was thoroughly searched. He looked at every tree trunk, searching for a moccasin, a fringe from an elbow, an irregular shadow, an alarmed bird or rodent, anything that would reveal a visitor. Again, nothing, now to the side opposite his seat and to the left of Clancy, he pushed a knee into the soft earth of the bank to give him greater height for his search. He felt something, and lifting his rifle to his shoulder he again used the barrel to point in the direction of his sight to ensure he didn't miss anything. A shadow moved, Caleb caught his breath, and looked through squinted eyes.

Suddenly two screaming warriors were charging directly at the startled figures partially hidden in the shallow gully. Their screams were terrifying and the painted faces were meant to strike fear into the heart of any opponent. Because their targets were mostly obscured, the warriors chose to attack, one with a lance and the other with a tomahawk.

With his heart beating double-time, Caleb eared back

the hammer, set the rear trigger and squeezed off the front trigger. The cloud of blue smoke chased the .54 caliber ball to its target and obscured the figure that was blasted off his feet to fall dead on his back with his war cry muffled with blood.

From the side a streak of black flew through the air with a growl befitting a Grizzly as Two Bits took the throat and lower face of the second warrior in his maw of a mouth. The massive black mountain of fur bore his prey to the ground with his teeth sinking deep into the throat of the attacker. The warrior's screams of terror were muffled with the stinking breath of the black mountain that bore him to the ground. Kicking and thrashing against the monster that threatened to devour him, the warrior's struggles weakened. Shaking his jaws side to side, Two Bits ripped the throat and lower jaw from the blood spattered warrior.

The Crow warrior's feet kicked as his hands grabbed at the dirt and his muscles contracted one last time. Two Bits spit out his trophy, trotted over to a small patch of grass and rolled in it to eliminate the stench of death from his fur. Wiping his jowls in the grass as a last measure of grooming, he casually strolled back to the small gulley that held his friends. He stretched out at the feet of Clancy and dropped his chin between his paws, closing his eyes as if to return to dreamland. Clancy leaned down and patting the dog's head whispered, "Thank you, Two Bits, thank you, my friend." The huge animal raised his head and Caleb was certain the dog smiled at her.

The carnage that lay scattered before them painted somber expressions on the faces of both men. Silently they seated themselves on the large grey trunk of a long dead pine that lay at the edge of the clearing now marked with blood and the many dead. They pondered the scene and the task that fell to them as the only living beings now wrapped in the silence of the forest.

"We must bury the dead and show proper respect for them," said Shield.

"That ravine's banks are steep enough that if we drag them over there, we could cave in the sides and push some rocks over. Should make a good enough grave. We could mark it with their belongings," suggested Jeremiah, ". . . and, of course, we'd have to keep the two peoples separate. Can't have mortal enemies buried together."

"What do we do about the woman?"

"Tell ya what, you see if you can't catch up one of these horses roamin' around here, make a travois to carry her on, and we can take her back to camp and see if she's gonna make it. Think you can do that with your shoulder wound?" asked Jeremiah. "If you can do that, I'll drag the bodies to the ravine and cover 'em up. Then we can work together to get her on the travois and get her back to camp."

Shield nodded to Jeremiah and both men rose to their agreed upon tasks. It was easy for Jeremiah to separate the Crow from the Blackfeet by both their hair styles and their clothing, as well as their facial paint. The Blackfeet used darker paint, and often had dark or black tanned moccasins, while many of the Crow had top-knot hair styles and more bead work on their tunics. Although the differences seemed subtle, the nuances of styles and colors made the identification easier. With Shield's shoulder wound it would have been harder for him to move the bodies so the task of catching a horse and fashioning the travois fell to him.

Within a couple of hours, both men returned to the log for a short rest before tackling the task of moving the woman to the waiting travois. Shield had captured a blue roan mare that stood with her reins held in the death grip of the warrior that rode her to the battle. Now she stood patiently with the cumbersome travois draped over her withers and trailing behind her. Her docile nature was unusual for a war pony of a warrior. Most often the ponies chosen by a warrior would be a high-strung animal that relished the opportunity to join in any conflict The excitement of battle and would add to the rush of adrenaline for the warrior that rode atop such an animal. But to have a calm manner and docile nature was unusual, indeed.

After a brief rest and an agreement on how to proceed, the two men walked to the berth in the bushes to retrieve the woman warrior and the leader of the Crow raiding party, Pine Leaf. Making their way into the thick brush they noted that the woman still lay unconscious and unmoving in the cradle of willows, but her breathing was evident and reassuring to the would-be rescuers.

With much awkward maneuvering and clumsy steps, the men carefully negotiated their way to the edge of the clearing and the waiting stretcher. The travois was cushioned by several blankets taken from the backs of other horses that had fallen in the battle and she was made as comfortable as possible.

The late afternoon sun illumined the floor of the high mountain valley giving Caleb a clear view of the entire panorama of the lush green meadow below him. Clancy stood by his side as the two ensured they were obscured by the cluster of tall pines at the tree line. They expected the two men to return before this and were concerned by their absence. Jeremiah had cautioned them to remain in the sheltered copse until they returned, but both youngsters were a little apprehensive at the uncertainty of the men's return and didn't like the idea of staying in the ravine and staring at the bodies of the slain warriors that lay a short distance from their haven. Caleb had made the decision to go to the tree-line to afford them a better view of the valley and enable them to prepare for whatever might come their way.

Shield led the way leading the blue roan bearer of the travois and Pine Leaf. They had to take the trail back to the fork and switch back to make it into the valley that held their camp. Most of the day was spent when they finally broke into the open after crossing the shallow Shoshone creek and headed for their campsite in the trees on the opposing hillside. When Caleb spotted the men, he was surprised at the unfamiliar sight of the blue roan and the travois, but immediately recognized Shield as the one leading the horse and his father bringing up the rear.

Caleb stepped from the trees and waved at the returning warriors, then returned to their campsite to stir up the coals and rekindle the fire. None of them had taken the time for a meal since they parted ways after breakfast and he knew the men would be just as hungry as he was. Clancy joined him in the preparations as they sliced off strips of the hanging hind quarter of deer that hung from the nearby tree. Taking the previously used willows, they speared the strips of meat and suspended each one over the growing flames. Clancy was busy stirring up a batch of cornbread to make some skillet fried cornpone.

As the men came into camp, Clancy turned to observe their preparation of the small lean-to and the bed for the wounded warrior. As they lifted her from the travois, she was startled to recognize Pine Leaf as the one that threw the lance that killed her mother. Her quick intake of breath caught the attention of Jeremiah as he watched her put her hand to her mouth and with a slight cry say, "She killed my mother! She threw the lance that killed my mother!"

Quickly she looked at Jeremiah and then to Caleb as if expecting them to do something then standing and looking at the prone figure now lying on the blanket bed in the lean-to, she said again, "She killed my mother!" as she slapped her legs with her hands in a show of both anger and frustration.

Jeremiah stepped before her and placing his hands on her shoulders, he said, "She probably did, but she is gravely wounded and still might die. She was a leader of the Crow and we must do all we can to help her. If she lives, she could be the one that will determine if our village can live here in peace. What she did was an act that will probably take you a long time to understand and you might not ever get over it, but you are a very brave and smart young woman and I believe you can be strong enough to get through this. Will you try to do that?"

She had looked at him all the while he was talking and trying to understand what he was saying, but the image of her mother grasping at the lance buried in her chest would not leave her. Now she dropped her gaze and mumbled, "I'll try, but I ain't promisin' nuthin'."

While Caleb and Clancy returned to their duties of preparing the meal, Jeremiah stepped to the side of Shield. The two men had both picked different plants as they moved along the trail during their return to the camp and now assembled their batch to prepare their remedies. Jeremiah had picked several hands full of rose hips and petals as well as some leaves and stems of Miner's lettuce.

Shield had gathered some leaves of Chickweed, pulled roots of fireweed and grabbed several Hound's Tongue leaves. While they separated their gatherings Jeremiah looked at the seeping wound in Shield's shoulder. It appeared the bullet had passed cleanly through just below the collar-bone and exited above the clavicle in his back. With no bones broken, the wound should quickly heal. Jeremiah said, "Looks like we need to cauterize your wound so we can get it to quit bleeding. Probably need to do the same to the woman. Then we can put these poultices on the wounds and get the two of you on the way to healing."

Thinking of the red-hot knife blade that would cauterize the wound, Shield begrudgingly agreed with a deep-throated grunt, then said, "Let's at least get somethin' to eat first. Every time I've seen somebody with a wound cauterized they passed out. So, I'd just as soon pass out with a full belly, if that's all right with you."

Jeremiah smiled, chuckled, and said, "I 'spose that's all right. I guess it won't hurt anything."

Pine Leaf was still unconscious when they prepared to work on her wound. After washing the wound front and back, Shield sat behind her, rested her against his chest and held her securely as Jeremiah pulled his knife from the fire. As he pressed the cherry red blade to her wound it seared and sizzled as smoke rose and carried the stench of burning flesh.

She uttered a scream and fought to escape the pain, then dropped back into unconsciousness. Shield quickly leaned her forward to expose the exit wound which Jeremiah swiftly cauterized. Shield then applied a poultice of the blend of crushed chickweed, fireweed roots and crushed Miner's lettuce to both the front and back then covered the poultices with the leaves of Hound's tongue and wrapped the entire shoulder with buckskin salvaged from an old tunic. Laying her back on the blanket under the lean-to, Shield then looked to Jeremiah knowing his friend waited to tend his wound.

Shield seated himself on the blankets beside the lean-to and prepared himself for the same ministrations just given to Pine Leaf. Jeremiah had returned his knife to the flames and now prepared similar poultices for Shield. After thoroughly cleaning the wound and wiping it dry, he looked at his friend and asked, "Are you ready for this?"

Shield nodded his assent and prepared himself for the coming pain. Jeremiah withdrew the glowing knife from the flame and as Shield bent forward, he applied the red-hot blade to the open wound. The searing and cooking of the flesh raised a stench unlike any other and Shield straightened up in shock but did not make a sound. Jeremiah replaced his knife in the fire and administered the poultice and leaves to the exit wound, looked Shield in the eyes and nodded his head for his friend to lay down. Jeremiah repeated the same procedure and quickly wrapped the shoulder and rolled Shield onto his back. His friend had also passed out and Jeremiah knew it would probably be morning before either of his patients stirred to wakefulness.

THE RISING SUN WAS JUST BEGINNING TO PAINT THE tree-tops on the western slope of the valley with golden rays of morning brightness when the smell of coffee brewing brought Jeremiah awake. The sudden moment of wakefulness filled his mind with the events of the previous day and night and he rolled from his blankets to check on his patients. Clancy Mae had surprised the camp with her early rising and starting the coffee.

She moved silently among the scattered packs searching for the makings for biscuits and a pan to prepare and cook them. With a glassy stare she remembered the many mornings shared with her momma as the two fixed her father's favorite biscuits. Remembering her momma's voice saying, "Your Da sure likes his crumpets wid his taa," brought a smile to her face and a tear to her eye. Wiping the tear away, she dug through the supplies thinking about what she would have to do to make something similar.

With biscuits in Ireland being more like cookies, and

crumpets more like a bread, she resolved to try to modify the usual cornpone into something new and tasty. Much of what she was doing was busywork to keep her mind off the woman warrior in the shelter that Clancy remembered as the one that launched the lance that stole the life of her mother.

She looked up as Jeremiah walked past the packs on his way to check on his patients.

Dropping to one knee, Jeremiah carefully lifted the bandage on Shield's shoulder causing Shield to open his eyes but not move. He was still weak from the wound and the treating of the injury. Jeremiah was expressionless as he examined his friend's shoulder, then looking at Shield said, "It's lookin' purty good. I think you just might live after all," with a droll grin.

"And here I was thinking about walking in the clouds with my ancestors."

"Don't go gettin' your hopes up about no cloud walkin'," said Jeremiah as he turned to look at the cloudless sky of the early morning, "cuz the clouds are a little scarce today. You'd just take a couple steps and fall right back down here and I'd have to patch you up again."

Shield turned to look at the still form of Pine Leaf and watched her slow breathing, noting she was still unconscious. "Have you looked at her wound yet?" he asked as he motioned to the woman warrior with his chin.

"Ain't had a chance, I was takin' care of the big sissy here," he chuckled.

Stepping to the shelter, Jeremiah leaned over the woman and reached for the bandage on her shoulder but was startled as she grabbed his hand before he touched her. With a malevolent stare, her wide eyes gave him an unmistakable warning. Jeremiah had stopped moving and did not force his movement but just looked directly at her without any alarm showing on his face.

She slowly released her grip and allowed him to lift the bandage to survey the wound. The exit wound from the musket ball of the Blackfeet was at the top edge of her right breast and was half the size of her palm. The cauterizing left an irregular shaped scab but had sealed the wound nicely. By motioning his intentions, he lifted her up to examine the entrance wound in her back. He would need to prepare more poultices and bandages to re-apply to both wounds.

He lay her back gently and made her understand his intentions with a combination of signs and the few words he knew of the Crow language. To his surprise she responded, "Do what you must, but I will be prepared to kill you if I need to."

"Well, ain't you just a bundle of joy this morning. That kinda talk won't get you any better doctorin' but if you was a little nicer, I might be a little gentler," he advised.

Turning back to Shield he said, "I think we got enough of them plants to make some more poultices, but we'll have ta' git some more soon. You two just lay there an' don't bother yourselves none and I'll pretend I know what I'm doin'."

Jeremiah rose and went to fetch a cup of coffee before starting the task of preparing the poultices. He asked Clancy to take some coffee to the two patients and offered to watch her skillet bread while she delivered the coffee. On her return he made his way to the collection of plants they gathered the previous day and sorted them out to start the preparations for the poultices and bandages. While he worked, he began to ponder what they would have to do in the coming days.

It would be necessary to get started back to the village as soon as possible for the people to begin the return trek to their proposed winter camp. But the complication of Shield's wound and the presence of Pine Leaf seemed to confound the thinking and planning. Shield could probably make the trip, although it wouldn't be easy, but it would take some time before Pine Leaf would be able to sit a horse and make any lengthy journey, even if it was wise to take her back to the Arapaho village.

They certainly couldn't take her to the Crow village as just getting anywhere near the Crow encampment could be life threatening. Especially if the Crow thought it was their doing that caused Pine Leaf's injury.

Jeremiah knew they would be safe where they were as he was certain there would not be any more raiding parties from either the Crow or the Blackfeet. He also thought he would have to replenish their meat supply as well as gather more medicinal plants. He continued the assembling of the plants and started crushing some roots and leaves with the same stones of the previous day. As was common with Jeremiah, he did his best thinking while busy with his hands and he began to form a plan for the coming days.

He returned to his patients and redressed the wounds, securing the poultices with the same buckskin patches. Shield rolled over, pushed himself to his hands and knees, then using the front pole of the lean-to, rose to his feet. Looking down at Jeremiah, still on his knees beside Leaf, he said, "I'm hungry. What's that girl fixin' over there cuz it's makin' my stomach growl like a grizzly!"

He walked to the fire and seated himself on a large stone within reach of the coffee pot and refilled his cup with the strong brew. Jeremiah had followed within arm's length to be certain his friend didn't eat a dust pie before he made it to the fire. He also seated himself and poured some more coffee. Turning to Clancy he said, "You made some right fine coffee this morning girl. I could get used to this and what's that you got goin' in the skillet thar?"

"We didn't have much left in fixins' so I had to make do with what we got. It's sorta like a cornpone only maybe a bit sweeter."

"Well, why don'tcha take a chunk o' that and some more coffee up to the woman yonder?" asked Jeremiah.

"She killed my mother!" spat Clancy, and turned to retreat to the trees, followed by Caleb.

Jeremiah and Shield looked at each other and Jeremiah said, "I guess I'm elected to feed the woman then."

"Give me the bread and coffee and I'll take it to her. I don't think she likes you very much, white man," he smiled.

"Oh, so you think you're gonna win her over with your smooth talkin' do ya?"

With a grunted response, Shield carried the vittles to the lean-to and dropped to his knees to assist the woman. He lifted her up and placed additional blankets behind her to enable her to be elevated enough to eat and drink.

Her eyes followed his every move and then she gruffly asked, "Where are my weapons?"

"Right over there," motioned Shield with a nod of his head, "but you're not in any condition to use them. You lost a lot of blood and it will take many days before you will be able to get around."

"You don't have me tied, why?"

"You're not a captive. We brought you here from the site of the battle and tended your wounds."

"My warriors, where are they?" she asked with a furtive glance around the camp.

"Dead, as are all the Blackfeet."

"All of them?" she inquired with fear in her eyes.

"White Wolf said there were two or three that ran, but the bushes were too thick to tell if they were Crow of Blackfeet. But they are long gone."

Her shoulders drooped as the words pierced her thoughts. Any war leader that lost all their men would never be a war leader again. A cloud of despair settled on her as she thought of the futility of returning to a village that would fault her for losing so many warriors. Her entire village would be weakened with the loss and they would be more vulnerable to attack from their enemies, the Blackfeet and the Sioux and even the Cheyenne.

Even her father, Black Buffalo, would be shamed by her failure. She looked at Shield as he held the skillet bread out to her, she started to lift her left hand but was too weak. The brief exertion against Jeremiah when he checked her bandages had tired her and she now breathed heavily and looked to Shield for help. He held the bread to her mouth as she struggled to take a bite.

After she swallowed, he held the cup of warm coffee so she could wash down the bread with the stimulating brew. With just a couple more bites and a last sip of coffee, she leaned back and closed her eyes to drop into a deep sleep.

When Shield returned to the fire he said to Jeremiah, "She is very weak. It will take many days before she can do much. She will not be able to ride for at least a week, maybe longer."

"That's what I was thinkin', and we ain't got that much time. The village needs to get started up here to make winter camp before the snow falls," answered Jeremiah as he looked up at Shield.

As Shield observed his friend, he could tell there was something on his mind or he was puzzling over a problem by the wrinkles in his forehead. He knew his long-time companion would work out every possible solution to any problem before he presented his plan or idea, and now the clouded expression showed he was a little troubled with his thoughts.

Jeremiah set his cup down on the rocks around the fire, stood and stretched. Looking at Shield, he began. "The way I see it, we can't take that woman with us and she can't travel anyway. But we need to get back to the village to get them started out this way without wastin' any more time. So, how 'bout you stayin' here with her, takin' care of her and all, and I'll take the younguns and go get the village. You'll both probably be all healed up by the time we get back and then we can decide what to do with her. Whatdaya think?"

Shield's mind had been traveling in the same direction and he also could find no other solution to the problem. He was reluctant to stay behind, but knew he would be the better choice because of his own wound and because Pine Leaf was well known to have nothing but hatred for any white man. Jeremiah was more than capable of returning to the village and leading them back to the chosen winter camp and his wife, Laughing Waters, would be a great help to him. He begrudgingly agreed, "What you say does seem to be the only answer."

"You'll need some more meat and some more medicine plants, so I'll take a jaunt and see what I can get for you. If I can get what you need and get back, we could even leave by mid-day. I figger to take a trail across the valley without goin' back around and I don't think I need to worry about another Crow raidin' party too soon. Of course if one o' them that got away was a Crow, he might be a little upset 'bout losin' all his friends."

"Then you need to get started soon," replied Shield.

The newly skinned carcass of a young buck hung from the high branch of the towering ponderosa at the edge of the clearing. It could be easily lowered with the rope whenever Shield would need to slice off a meal's worth of meat, and just as easily raised above the reach of any prowling predators that would be brave enough to attempt a midnight theft.

Jeremiah had also gathered a sufficient quantity of the medicinal plants for making poultices for the wound dressings and had also left additional buckskin for more bandages. They were able to spare some of the cornmeal and other supplies that would tide them over until the expected return of his friend and the rest of the village.

With a foot in the stirrup, Jeremiah hefted his bulk astride his steel-dust gelding and turned to face the waiting Shield. "Your horses, including that sorrel that wandered in, are still tethered over yonder on that patch of grass in the clearing and they should be alright for the rest of the day. They can get to the water in that spring-fed stream that runs across the corner there before it gets down here. I know I don't have to give you any advice, but keep your head down, anyway."

Shield sported a wide grin as he lifted his hand to send Jeremiah and the youngsters on their way with a wave. As the trio kneed their mounts to start for the trail, Shield said, "As you drop off into the valley, use that far-off flat top butte as a marker. Bear to the north of it and you will cross the river just beyond."

"I ain't no pilgrim, I can find my way back. We'll be back before ya know it!" replied Jeremiah over his shoulder as they disappeared through the trees below the clearing and the camp.

Looking around the meadow from within the tree-line, he led the way toward the trail leading into the site of the battle. The plan was to follow the path to the point of land that jutted out below the tall craggy granite peaks of the last of the Absaroka, and cut straight across the semi-barren stretch of valley that cradled the winding Wind River as it carved its way southeast.

His home was nestled in the tall timber on the shoulder of foothills of the Wind River Mountain Range, and he was anxious to see his wife, Laughing Waters.

THE EARLY AFTERNOON SUN CAST A LAZY HAZE ON the winding trail that snaked its way through the scrub oak and into the fingers of pine making its way slowly down the western slope of the Absaroka Range.

Jeremiah led the way leading the pack mule and was trailed by Clancy Mae on the Blue Roan that had pulled the travois to the camp while Caleb brought up the rear. This beginning of the homeward trek seemed to still the conversation while each became immersed in their individual reverie. Jeremiah allowed his mind to wander back to his newly built home and he pictured their hideaway clearing filled with brush arbors, teepees, and other shelters with the many villagers that had fled from the destruction of the recent fire.

He knew Waters would be busy assisting her father, Black Kettle, as they ministered to the many injured. Their winter store of meat was probably quickly diminishing but Jeremiah held no animosity toward those that needed the sustenance. It would just mean more hunting trips when they settled into their winter camp.

He thought about the coming winter, *Maybe I'll have to build another cabin up there. I can't have my growing family sleeping out in the open in that high meadow. I'm sure the winter's up there will be plumb miserable. Hmmm . . .and I'll probably need to make it bigger now that Clancy Mae's gonna be part of our family.*

He pictured the expression on Water's face when she saw the new addition to the family. He was confident she would just smile and say something about letting him go off by himself again and bringing back another foundling. She had already shown what a great mother she was by her adopting Caleb and they both were anxiously awaiting the birth of their first child that should come sometime in the fall. He forced himself to focus on the present as the easy rocking gait of his steel-dust lulled him into complacency.

Clancy Mae sat comfortably astride the blue roan mare, although without a saddle, she was content with the pad of blankets and the stirrups made from the long latigo straps. Before her family left their home for this new adventure, she had often ridden her family's saddle horse bareback on her many forays into the nearby woods. She reached down and patted the neck of the mare and spoke softly to her. "I think I'm gonna call you Blue Moon. Yeah, that's a good name for you, you're my Blue Moon. Momma would've liked you, girl. She always wanted a horse of her own."

The thoughts of her mother brought tears to her eyes. Although she loved her father, he was often away on his own for whatever reason he could come up with and Clancy and her mother spent many hours together sharing every dream and idea that a young girl could imagine. It was the image of her mother standing in the wagon with the lance buried in her chest that Clancy could not erase and each remembrance of it brought a mixture of emotions roaring into her mind and heart and always brought a flood of tears streaming their way down her freckled face.

Wiping the tears on her sleeve, she slapped her hand to her thigh in anger and startled the mare to a quick jump that, in turn, scared Clancy Mae but she quickly recovered and drew the mare up to a walk.

"What're ya' doin' up there, girl... are ya tryin' ta' get bucked off or what?" shouted Caleb.

"No! I was just wakin' up my horse and me too. It was so quiet, we were both tryin' to go to sleep," she answered back over her shoulder.

"Well, don't go makin' too much noise, ya might wake up all them sleepin' Crow!"

"Where?" she shouted as she searched the surrounding trees for any sign of attack.

"All those my Pa buried back there," he said, motioning to the rear where the battle had taken place.

"Well if they're buried, they can't hear enough to wake up anyway!" she said with finality in her voice and a firm "Humph" to stem any further comment.

Caleb retreated into his own pensive mood thinking about how his life had made so many twists and turns in his few years. He often spent time remembering his Mom and Dad and even his Step-Mom and his early life in

Michigan. But when he compared those early years with the more recent times in the mountains, he knew he much preferred his present life. However, that didn't mean he didn't miss his family, but he loved his uncle Jeremiah and his new Mom, Laughing Waters, and now it appeared he had gained a sister in Clancy Mae.

I wonder how things are gonna change with her around? It might be fun havin' her as a sister, she don't seem so bad, for a girl. Maybe he could teach her all about gettin' along in the woods and about animals and such. Maybe Black Kettle could make her a bow like he did for me and then we could go huntin' with 'em. Yeah, that might be alright. He never imagined he'd have a sister, and he was just getting used to the idea of being a brother what with the new baby coming. The idea of being a part of such a big family was a little overwhelming.

The last couple of miles of the trail had a considerable descent causing the riders to lean way back on their mounts as the horses picked their footing on the rocky trail. There were occasional large boulders resting in the middle of the trees with no other stones around them that caused the travelers to wonder how the boulder ended up in the middle of trees. Usually there would be a path that revealed the route of the rockslide that released the boulder from a higher promontory, but these rested in places as if some giant hand had plucked them from some other location and gently placed them among the trees just to make people marvel. And marvel they did. Caleb spoke up and asked, "Pa, how'd those boulders get there in the middle of those trees?"

As Jeremiah looked at the boulders, he just shrugged

and said, "I guess God did that just to make you ask questions."

"Hmmm, well I asked the question, but you ain't givin' me any answers," chuckled the boy. Both Jeremiah and Caleb heard the mumbled comment from Clancy Mae, "There ain't no God anymore."

Stunned to silence, father and son returned their attention to the trail and continued to rock their hips in harmony to the cadence of the horses making their way down the steep trail. As the trail began to level out, it was evident they were approaching the edge of the trees and Jeremiah looked around for a likely campsite for the night. Away from the trail about fifty feet, he spotted an open grassy area next to a cascading small stream that fought its way down the mountainside. Motioning his followers to join him, he turned from the trail to the clearing and began the chores of making camp.

"We're not goin' ta have a fire tonight. We're still in Crow territory and I don't want to do anything to tell 'em we're here. We can manage with a cold camp. We'll git some rest tonight, get on our way in the mornin' and have a better camp tomorrow night," stated Jeremiah as he busied himself dropping the packs from the mule and unsaddling his horse.

The two youngsters followed suit and when the horses were free of tack, Caleb and Clancy led them to the upper corner of the clearing to a greener patch of grass and within reach of the stream. Jeremiah had already tethered his horse and mule and returned to the lower and more level part of the clearing to ready his bedroll. Their stop for the camp was determined as much by the location as the time of day, Jeremiah didn't want to be caught in the middle of the open spaces of the Wind River valley with nothing for protection but sagebrush. After the two youngsters had rolled out their bedding, Jeremiah suggested to Caleb that this would be a good opportunity to catch up on some of his reading.

"Reading? You mean like schoolwork?" asked Clancy Mae.

"Yeah, sorta. It's kind of an agreement we have. Since we don't have any other school books for his education, we use the Bible for just about all of it. When it talks about numbers, like how many cubits in the Ark and such, we work on our sums. And when it talks about different countries, we talk about geography and land formations and such. And, of course, the reading takes care of itself," explained Jeremiah.

"We didn't do much Bible reading around my house. I guess it don't make no difference anyhow, ya can't believe what it says anyway," she said with a pout.

Jeremiah knew the thoughts that Clancy Mae harbored because of her recent loss and knowing she never really had the time to grieve, he understood the conflicting emotions that caused her struggle. He also knew that folks often expressed opinions that came more from emotion rather than from reason. Sometimes it was best to let the expressions work themselves out rather than trying to argue the point. However, the evident heartbreak that lingered just below the surface for this young girl could cause irreparable harm if not resolved.

"I have found that even in my darkest moments, and when I think God has abandoned me, He will make

Himself known when I least expect it. Maybe it'll be in a beautiful sunset, or some comforting event or word, or maybe in the truth of the Scripture. You know, Clancy, what you have experienced is a very great loss, but that doesn't mean that God doesn't love you or that He has forsaken you. I believe that God brought us to you and you to us for a very special reason."

"What reason is that, and why couldn't He protect my Momma?" she sneered.

"Did your Momma and Dad know Christ as their Savior?" Jeremiah asked.

"They believed in God and read the Bible and all that, and back home we went to church all the time, but it didn't do any good," she responded and continued, "and what'dya mean know Christ?"

"That means to do like it says in Romans chapter 10, *"For whosoever shall call upon the name of the Lord, shall be saved."* Or to fully believe with all your heart and ask Him to be your Savior. That's more than just believing that there is a God, that's trusting Him with all that you are or will be."

"You mean if I do that, then everything will be all right and I won't have any more problems?" she asked.

With a bit of a chuckle, Jeremiah responded, "Well, we'll always have problems, but it does mean that He'll be your Savior and when the time comes, you'll get to spend eternity in Heaven with Him."

"So is my Momma in Heaven?" she asked with imploring eyes.

"If she trusted Jesus as her Savior, yes she is."

"So, how do I do that? Trust Him as Savior, I mean."

"Well, if you mean it with all your heart, all you have to do is say a prayer and ask Him to come into your heart and be your Savior. That's what it means when it says, *"Whosoever shall call. . ."*

"I'll think about it. But I'm still mad cuz He didn't save my Mum."

"Clancy, I lost my Dad and my Mom and then I lost my Step-Mom too. But God has taken care of me and given me a new Mom and Dad," interjected Caleb.

"Well, I don't have a new Mom and Dad, so what about me? Doesn't He love me?" she pleaded.

"Clancy, if you would let us, my wife and I would like to be your new Mom and Dad," stated Jeremiah with a degree of tenderness that even he didn't know he had.

Clancy Mae dropped her head to look at her bedroll, then tried to wipe away some tears without her two companions noticing. She then turned around, straightened out her bedroll and mumbled over her shoulder, "I'm tired. I'm goin' to sleep. Good night."

Two Bits raised his head in a lazy but curious move as he watched Clancy Mae walk from the clearing into the nearby trees. The dim light of early morning was just enough for the travelers to start packing up and saddle the horses in preparation of the day's journey. Clancy retreated to the cover of trees for her personal business and Two Bits continued to stare in her direction. Just a few minutes had passed when the men were startled by a scream from the trees.

Two Bits jumped to his feet and leaped toward the girl as she came running from the trees, looking back over her shoulder and screaming, "Bear, bear, it's a bear!"

Jeremiah had grabbed his Hawken at the first cry of alarm and now covered the distance to the girl in four long strides. Caleb also grabbed his rifle and turned to the point of alarm. Two Bits was barking and growling at the edge of the trees as a large black bear rose to its two hind legs and with a massive head tilting to the side let loose a guttural roar that seemed to shake the cones from the pines.

Two Bits raced around the bear and took a stand in front of it and barked and growled to match the bear, threat for threat. The repeated barking of the dog seemed to confuse the bear as it swatted at nothing to the front and side attempting to catch the dog with its threatening claws. Jeremiah lowered his rifle to take aim at the intruder, but a glimpse to the side caught two miniature versions of the behemoth scrambling up a nearby tree. Jeremiah motioned Clancy to get behind him and turned to Caleb, "Son, don't shoot her, that's a momma bear that's protecting her cubs. You take a shot just over her head at the tree trunk behind her, maybe that'll scare her enough. I'll save my load just in case."

Caleb quickly aimed over the head of the bear and squeezed off a shot. The blast of the rifle and the accompanying cloud of blue smoke alarmed the bear and she ceased her growling. The continual barking and growling of the monster dog before her and the confusing noise of the rifle shot prompted her to drop to all fours and tuck her stub of a tail, lope to the tree with her cubs and with a mother's warning to them, the three ambled off into the woods with the momma bear looking over her shoulder at the intruders into her world.

"Now I 'spose you're gonna say that God was takin' care of me," blurted Clancy belligerently.

With a low chuckle and a smile, Caleb responded, "Well, think what mighta happened if that bear had taken after you before we were here. Then what would you have done?"

"I'd a run a lot faster, that's what!"

Having their nerves strung as tight as a banjo string set the trio on the trail a bit quicker than normal. All were glad to put some distance between them and the momma bear, just in case she changed her mind and went looking for vittles for her young ones.

It promised to be a long day as the sun rose with all its blazing glory unhindered by a single cloud. The blue sky seemed to go on forever and the mountains that were their destination were but miniscule images and only ripples on the far horizon. The terrain before them was endless rolling plains with scattered sagebrush, buffalo grass, and dry dusty swales between undulating hillocks and often laced with deeper flood-formed washouts and gullies.

In the distance, about thirty miles, rose a large flat-top butte that served as a prominent landmark for the lowland of the Wind River valley. It marked the half-way point to their destination and home. By pushing their mounts, they should make it to the butte and maybe find some shelter for the night.

With the open spaces before them the two youngsters chose to ride side by side, making conversation easier. Clancy had been in a rather quiet mood but now opened up with a question for Caleb. "You never said how you lost your Mum and Da and your step-mom. What happened and how old were you?"

Caleb freely opened up about his past and shared all the details of the plague that hit his hometown area and how his father, a doctor, had cared for everyone and was eventually taken himself and then his step-mom also died.

"Why weren't you angry about that? I sure woulda been," she replied.

"I was, but my step-mom had prayed for an answer, and in walked Jeremiah, her brother. She never thought she'd see him again, but she said he sure was an answer to prayer. Then when he and Scratch got to talkin' about the mountains and such, it just seemed like it was meant to be, and you could say, I ain't looked back."

"Are you happy with your new Mum and Da?"

"Sure am! They're the best, and Laughing Waters is the best mom a guy could have. She can outshoot Pa with a bow and she's taught me a lot." His enthusiasm overflowed with a big smile on his face as he thought about his life with Jeremiah and Waters. "I think it'd be great to have you as a sister too, even though you are a girl."

"Silly, if I wasn't a girl, I wouldn't be a sister, now would I?"

"Uh, no, I guess not. That's all right, I won't hold it against ya."

"Do you think Laughing Waters will like me?" she asked, with concern etched on her forehead.

"Sure she will, and I bet the first thing she'll do, after huggin' and kissin' on ya, will be to make you a buckskin outfit like she did for me," he grinned.

Jeremiah turned to the youngsters and suggested to Caleb, "Hey son, why don't you take Clancy up ahead there to that bit of a knoll and see if you can't spot a deer or an antelope for our supper? Think you can do that?"

"Sure Pa," he replied then turned to Clancy and said, "Come'on sis, let's go get us an antelope."

The two hunters gigged their horses past Jeremiah and trotted to the indicated knoll. Caleb motioned to Clancy to pull up before they crested the hillock. They both dropped from their mounts and tied them off to a tall sagebrush. Making their way silently to the crest, Caleb motioned for them to drop down on all fours, then to their bellies before they reached the top of the knoll. He whispered, "If there's anything over there, we gotta be quiet and move slowly. Pa says they got eyesight better'n ours and can see even the slightest movement."

Following Caleb's example, Clancy followed with a belly crawl to peek over the crest. Less than one hundred yards away stood several antelope with both bucks and does and even a couple of fawns. "It'd be best to take a doe, but we don't want one that's got a fawn by her side. Ya' see one?"

"How do you tell the difference? They all look the same to me."

"The bucks are those bigger ones with the bigger horns out there to the side, see? They're keepin' watch for the herd," he pointed. "The does are a little smaller, horns not quite as big, and they hang out with the rest of the bunch. See if you can spot one that ain't got a fawn by her side."

As she scanned the small herd, she noticed one just a short way away from the herd and all by her lonesome. "There, that one on the left there. Is she one?"

"Yeah, looks good. That should be an easy shot, too. Ya wanna take it?"

"Me? Shoot your rifle? Are you sure?"

"Haven't you ever shot one before?"

"Yeah, I have."

"O.K. then, here ya go," he said as he slid his rifle over to her. "It's got double set triggers, so as you cock the hammer you set it with the back trigger, then when you're ready, squeeze it off with the front trigger."

She slowly brought the Hawken to her shoulder, sighted down the barrel lining the front blade with the rear buckhorn sight, then pulled back the hammer setting it with the rear trigger, re-lined her sights, took a breath and squeezed off. The click of the cocking action brought up the head of the watchful buck but before he could alarm the herd, the Hawken roared its thunder and spat its plume of smoke. The two hunters rose to their elbows and looked at the herd that was disappearing in the distance and spotted the prone antelope between the two shrubs of sagebrush.

"You got it! Good shootin' sis!" proclaimed Caleb with pride. "Now the work begins. You fetch the horses and I'll check on your kill. We gotta gut her out before she starts spoilin' in this heat."

As Clancy returned to the horses, Jeremiah arrived to see the broad smile on her face. Having heard the report of the rifle, he knew they shot at something and now inquired, "What'd he get?"

"He didn't get nothin', I did! I got an antelope!" she proudly proclaimed with her hands on her hips and a smile on her face.

"You did? Well, I declare. Now we got another hunter in the family. That's great. Come'on then, let's go get it and pack it up so we can get on to make camp and have some fresh meat for supper." With a broad smile, he turned his mount to follow Clancy to help the two hunters with their prize.

As dusk settled in, the travelers were watching the strips of fresh Antelope meat sizzling over the fire. As so often happens, the crackling fire caused empty stares to linger on the dancing flames and reminisce about the days' travel and successful hunt. The tall butte towered over them as they settled into their camp between the two finger ridges coming off the butte. It promised to be a restful night as they all anticipated arriving home by this time tomorrow.

THE TOWERING BUTTE HELD THE TRIO IN THE cooler shadows of early morning as the rising sun struggled to paint the valley with golden rays. With the gray of dawn yielding to the new day, the Wind River valley was an artist's palette of quickly retreating shadows clinging to scrub bunches of sage brush and the lone flat-top butte.

As the trio found their way around the west side of what would one day become known as Crow Heart butte, their eyes lingered on the green of the cottonwoods lining the shore of the distant Wind River. Clancy Mae noticed the lift in the spirits of both Jeremiah and Caleb and reckoned it to be because of the nearness of their home. She wondered about the reception she would get from this group of strangers, and at how she would adjust to living with Indians.

For the many months of traveling with those on the wagon train, the men her father befriended continually berated all Indians and referred to them as heathens and monsters. Her mother had always taught her that each individual should be treated with patience and under-standing, no matter their color or language or homeland. She had reminded Clancy Mae that they were visitors into this land and should treat everyone like she would want to be treated.

Looking down at the big black dog trotting beside her she quipped, "What are we gonna do, Two Bits? I like these two, but I dunno about the rest of 'em. What if they wanna scalp us? You better stick close to me boy, cuz I hear that Indians eat dogs, and you'd make a meal for a whole family!"

"Are you talkin' to yourself again?" asked Caleb. They were traveling single file again and Caleb was behind the girl when he called out his question.

"No! I'm talkin' to my dog," she said as she looked down at Two Bits, "Ain't I, boy?"

"That's only cuz he's the only one that won't argue with you! Course, Pa always said a man should never argue with a woman cuz he ain't ever gonna win."

"Then maybe you oughta start takin' his advice!"

"Always do!" he said as he kneed his roan in the ribs to prompt him to move alongside the girl. "Say, you know, as good as you did with that lucky shot on the antelope, I bet Waters will teach you how to use a bow and you'll probably get as good as me one day."

"Did you say, 'lucky shot'? I'll have you know, I have always been an excellent shot. My Da used to take me huntin' squirrel with him all the time and I never missed!"

"Yeah, but that's usin' a shotgun and anybody can hit a little bitty squirrel with a shotgun," he said as he turned away and cupped his hands to his mouth. He let go with a perfect imitation of the squirrel chuckle, repeated it, and put his hand behind his ear as if to listen.

Clancy Mae furrowed her brow and asked, "What are you doing?"

"Oh, just warnin' all the squirrels that the mighty squirrel hunter was comin' their way and they better hide out!"

With a groan of exasperation, Clancy responded, "Oh you! You can't talk to the squirrels!"

"Okay, just wait. We'll see if there are any squirrels when we get to the river or if they got the message and are hidin' out," he replied with a grin splitting his face.

It was still the first part of the morning when they arrived at the bank of the river. Even the morning sun was blistering and the continuing drought had made every step of the horses kick dust aloft. The shade of the tall cottonwoods was a welcome relief and just the sight of the cool waters of the river seemed to refresh them.

Across the stream, the trail skirted a short bluff that was about twice the height of the horses and obscured the sight of Jeremiah. He wasn't comfortable making them vulnerable crossing the river without knowing what was on the other side. The opposite riverbank held clusters of willow and alder and a few scattered stunted Cotton-wood. The near side seemed to hoard most of the taller trees and provide good cover and shelter, but across the way, the bluff could hide any number of dangers.

Turning back to the youngsters, he said, "You two stay here, hold on to the pack mule, and I'll signal you when to cross. We don't wanna take any unnecessary chances this close to home."

Caleb gigged his mount forward to take the lead rope for the mule and nodded at his Pa to indicate his understanding. With the lead rope in his left hand, he slipped his Hawken from its scabbard and laid it across his lap looking to the hammer and ensuring the cap was in place. With another nod to his Pa, he indicated his readiness. Jeremiah then started across the river. It was a good stone bottom and rather shallow crossing and he did not anticipate any problems with the stream so his attention was solely on the opposite shore. The steel-dust gelding carefully picked his steps across the river. The water was clear and it was easy to see any obstacles, but there were none.

It was an easy slope from the water making the exit from the river a couple of long steps from the tall gelding. His smooth stride allowed Jeremiah to continue to focus his attention on every possible hiding place within the scattered bushes lining the bank. A small, grassy area welcomed him and his horse stopped to shake the excess water off causing Jeremiah to grab at the saddle horn and comment, "What's the matter boy, I thought you'd like a refreshing bath?" Dusty bent his neck around and looked up at the man on the saddle as if to say, "You could use a bath too!"

With another look around, he turned and motioned to the youngsters to join him. Within a few moments, the kid's horses repeated the shaking action of the steel dust and elicited similar responses from their riders. The mule just watched with a look of disdain in his eyes and chose to just let the water drip off his muscular body. With his long legs, the water barely touched his belly while the two smaller mounts of the youngsters were in the water mid-rib deep. One rolling shake wasn't enough for them and as Caleb and Clancy dropped to the ground to stretch their legs, the horses exerted another effort to rid themselves of water by shaking again. Jeremiah said, "I'm gonna check out above that bluff real quick, you two just wait here."

The trail bent around a shoulder of the bluff and rose up the side of a small ravine to top out on a flat. Jeremiah noticed some fresh tracks on the trail ahead and slipped his Hawken from the scabbard, holding it across his lap. As the horse approached the crest of the bluff, he saw several dark wooly shapes scattered about the grassy knoll. Reining in his horse, he dropped to the ground, let his reins fall to ground tie his horse, and slowly moved the last few feet of the trail to observe the buffalo grazing on the sparse patches of drying grasses. *We could use some more meat for the village and ain't nuthin' better'n buffalo hump roast.* He knelt to one knee, using his left knee to rest his left elbow and provide a sturdy rest for his shot.

He was focused on a sizable cow that grazed by herself to the left of the rest of the herd. None of the herd seemed to notice him, but there was always a herd bull that had the responsibility of look-out but Jeremiah was focused on his intended kill. Aligning the front blade between the rear buckhorn sights, he casually cocked the hammer with the rear set trigger, then moved his finger to the smaller forward trigger. Slowly he squeezed and suddenly the thunder rocked him back as the blast stirred the dust in front of his barrel and the cloud of blue smoke erupted in the midst of the roar.

The bullet was true and a small cloud of dust erupted from just behind the massive head and the neck shot dropped the big cow before she could take a step. Jeremiah lifted his head to look over the slowly dissipating smoke to see if the shot was true, and a thunder that vibrated the ground beneath him quickly drew his attention to his right. Charging straight for him was a massive bull with his head lowered and fire in his eyes. Jeremiah was able to turn slightly toward the speeding threat but didn't have enough time to even take a single step to retreat.

The burly head struck him belt high and the bull threw his head up lifting the helpless man over his head in a somersault that landed him below the edge of the bluff face down into the adobe clay and powdery dust. The bull stepped to the edge and looked down at his victim that lay immobile below him, snorted an additional threat that stirred the dust at his feet, then tossing his head he turned and trotted off.

Caleb and Clancy heard the report of the rifle, and turned in that direction to see if Jeremiah appeared. What they saw was not what they expected as Jeremiah took flight over the edge of the bluff. They stood transfixed by the sight and were amazed at the size of the bull buffalo that stood at the edge of the bluff and then disappeared. Finally stirred to action, Caleb swung atop his roan and kicked him towards the bluff. Stopping on the trail below Jeremiah, he quickly dismounted and dug his toes into the side of the hill to make his way to his Pa. "Pa, Pa, are you O.K.? Speak to me Pa! Pa?"

Jeremiah groaned, started to roll over and slid down

the slope another short distance followed by Caleb, then he sat up with his left arm dangling to the side. With his right arm he felt his stomach and ribs, groaned again, tried to move his left arm and was startled by the pain. Looking down, he saw his forearm was bent at an unusual angle and realized it was broken.

Looking around, he asked Caleb, "Have you seen my rifle boy? Get my rifle, son, it might still be up top there so be careful." Caleb dug his toes into the soft sides of the bluff and made his way to the top. Peering over the crest, he spotted the Hawken and noticed the buffalo retreating in the distance. He also saw the downed cow buffalo about seventy yards distant. He picked up the rifle and slid down the slope to his Pa's side.

Looking at the way Jeremiah held his left arm, Caleb observed, "Well, it looks like you really did it this time."

Jeremiah couldn't help himself and started chuckling at the understatement of his son, knowing there were challenges ahead for all of them. "Yeah, you could say that, I guess. So, let's get to it, shall we? To start with, how 'bout you fetchin' my horse over here?" As Caleb went to get Dusty, Jeremiah stood up and carefully tucked his left hand behind his belt and stepped to the trail. As Caleb turned the mount around, Jeremiah grimaced in pain as he grabbed the saddle horn with his right hand and stepped up and mounted his horse.

Caleb handed him his rifle and he slipped it into the scabbard. Clancy had brought the mule and Caleb's roan forward with her and the boy quickly mounted, grabbed the mule's lead rope, and followed Clancy up the trail after Jeremiah. As they arrived at the downed buffalo carcass, Jeremiah began to give instructions but was interrupted by Caleb, "Before we start on that," motioning with his head, "don't you think we oughta do something about that?" pointing at his broken arm.

With a deep sigh, Jeremiah threw his leg over the rump of his horse and carefully dismounted. There was a scrawny snag of a white trunk dead cottonwood a couple of steps from the carcass and he sat down to lean against it. After explaining to the youngsters what they would need to do, he prepared himself with a short silent prayer and gritted his teeth.

Caleb sat down, carefully lifted his Pa's left hand with both of his, placed his moccasin-clad foot in the crook of the elbow and said, "How will I know if it's set right?"

"Well it should look straighter than it is and I think you'll know. Now, if I pass out, finish up, use those branches you gathered and secure the arm tightly with the buckskin, then just leave me be. I'll wake up soon enough. Oh, and skin out that buffalo there while you're at it," he grinned.

Without any warning, Caleb pulled and pushed on the arm, grunting with the exertion and watched as the skin stretched and the bone slid into place. Jeremiah gritted his teeth tighter and groaned with the pain, sweat beaded on his forehead and he held his breath. Caleb slowly released the pressure noting the bone staying in place, and grabbed for the splints and buckskin. Clancy handed the branches to be used for splints and the long wide strips of buckskin watching Jeremiah slowly take in a deep breath. Clancy carefully held the arm as Caleb wrapped the buckskin tightly around and around to secure the splints, then tied it off with the split ends of buckskin. Jeremiah leaned his head back and closed his eyes and began to breathe deeply. Caleb ripped the end of a blanket off to fashion a sling for his Pa's arm and returned to his side to drape it over his head and place the splinted limb inside.

With the previous buffalo hunt behind him, Caleb called on his brief experience to skin and butcher the big cow. Clancy was a willing student and the two of them looked like kids playing in a big red mud puddle by the time they were done. A quick trip back to the river to wash up and a final check of the load on the pack mule and the additional cuts behind the saddles of both Jeremiah and Caleb and the trio was once again on the trail. The buffalo incident had consumed about three hours of their travel time and Jeremiah knew it would be well after dark before they would arrive home, but he was determined to complete the trip without another night on the trail.

All were anxious to complete the journey, but the extra exertion of the butchering and the trauma with Jeremiah had tired them all and definitely increased their appetite. The growling bellies demanded they stop and refresh themselves as well as give their mounts a rest. Finding a likely spot as they neared the tree-line of the foothills, a little feeder creek provided fresh water for the mounts and refills for their water-bags.

Clancy made short work of getting a fire going and Caleb sliced off some fresh buffalo strips to hang over the fire. The shade of the pinion and juniper wasn't as cool as that near the river, but was still welcomed by the weary travelers. Enjoying the fresh meat as the juices dripped down their cheeks, the conversation was non-existent until the appetites were satisfied. Then Clancy asked the age-old question, "Are we there yet?"

THE SHADOWS FROM THE STUBBY PINIONS WERE lengthening as the day was drawing to a close. The trail turned to the southwest and pointed the travelers to the towering peaks of the Wind River Range. The dusk lessened the stifling heat of the day as the silent trio determined to reach their destination without another stop. The long gait of the pack mule pushed the steel-dust that carried an uncomfortable Jeremiah. Almost every step of his mount elicited a muffled moan as he began to feel the effects of his untimely meeting with the big buffalo.

He was certain he had several broken ribs and at the very least he figured the morning would see a black and blue body. With the rocking gait of his mount, the struggle of enduring the pain and his anxiousness of getting home, Jeremiah wasn't as attentive as usual. The sudden appearance of a figure in the middle of the trail before him and the unusual sound of "He he . . ." brought him up short. From behind him came a shout, "Uncle Scratch!"

Sitting astride a lop-eared paint colored mule was his old friend and long-time companion, Scratch. With a smile as wide as the horizon that peeked from under his scraggly beard and eyes that sparkled with mischief, the scruffy mountain man sat patiently waiting the arrival of his friends. As Jeremiah pulled alongside his friend, he said, "Why you ol' reprobate! What're you doin' up here in God's country? I thought you settled down with your woman an' was gonna sit on the porch and watch your younguns play in the mud puddles. Boy, it's good to see you," stated Jeremiah as he reached out his hand to greet his friend.

Scratch had noticed the injured arm in the sling and stopped his leaning in anticipation of a bear hug and extended his hand for a handshake greeting. "What happened to your wing thar boy? Fall off yore horse, didja?"

"Ha! He tried flying and had a sudden reckoning with the ground!" laughed Caleb from behind his Pa, doing little to stifle the laughter.

"Well, lookie at you, boy! I'll be snookered if you didn't grow up a mite!" observed Scratch, as he urged the mule alongside the boy's roan and reached over to swallow him in a bear-hug.

Jeremiah looked around to see if Scratch was alone, wondering where his woman was and hesitating to ask for fear of the wrong answer. When the two men were last together, they were parting ways at the end of the crossing with the wagon train. Scratch had decided to settle down with a woman that had joined them in the crossing of the territory from the Mississippi River to the western frontier.

When several of the members of the train chose to continue West, Scratch determined to go as far as the new trading post Jim Bridger was building and maybe help out his old friend. Both men were certain they would never see each other again this side of Heaven, and now here he was all by his lonesome. Jeremiah looked at his friend and with a questioning look and a nod of his head, Scratch knew what he was thinking.

"Nah, Charlie done decided the wilderness weren't fer her and when a handsome young peddler came along, she up and left with him without a 'by your leave' or nuthin'. She was just gone. So, I figgered I'd come up here an' see if you two were stayin' outta trouble." It was a combination of relief and frustration that showed on the face of the mountain man, but Jeremiah knew it was also a breath of freedom that stirred his friend to return to the mountains.

"Well, you're just in time. We gotta move a whole village of Arapaho to their winter camp a few days North of here, and with my busted up wing, I could use the help."

"A whole village?" implored Scratch.

As Jeremiah began to explain the many happenings of the season, the men started back up the trail to make use of the remaining daylight. The continual climb of the trail often interrupted the conversation as they were forced to move single file to negotiate the path. Yet as darkness draped its mantle on the travelers, they were nearing the crest of the foothills. The trail into the tall timber was easier traveling and the pace picked up as animals and travelers alike were anxious to reach the end of the trail and the rest that beckoned.

The three quarter moon shone down from a cloudless sky that displayed what appeared to be millions of stars with each pinpoint of light giving encouragement to the observers. The beauty of God's creation in the heavens above paraded across the arch of wonder over the heads of tired but appreciative travelers.

The dog soldier warriors were observant lookouts and had already passed the word to the village that White Wolf, Talks to the Wind and two others were nearing the village. As the travelers approached the clearing, several cook-fires had been rekindled to light the way. Waiting beside the trail at the edge of the clearing, Waters anxiously stood looking for her husband and son. As soon as the cavalcade cleared the trees, Jeremiah stopped his mount and dropped to the ground to greet Waters. She noticed his sling and bandaged arm and moved to his right side to reach up to his neck and pull his head down to hers so she could properly greet her husband with a welcome kiss.

As she looked at the rest of the group, she turned to Jeremiah and said, "It looks like you have much to talk about. I have your meal waiting for you. I will wait for you in our home." She then returned to the cabin while Jeremiah and the others tended to the horses and packs. Several of the villagers assisted them as they unpacked the buffalo meat and hide. One of the young warriors took their horses to the corral by the cabin and Jeremiah went to Black Kettle to tell of the new camp.

Caleb, Clancy Mae and Scratch went to the cabin while Jeremiah conversed with Black Kettle and the other leaders of the village. Caleb was excited to tell his Ma about his new sister and her new daughter and as he rambled on with all the details, Laughing Waters went to Clancy and wrapped her arms around her to embrace her with the kind of hug that only loving mothers can give. Displaying a smile that showed a genuine love and total acceptance, she held Clancy at arm's length and said, "If I could choose from all the girls in the world for a daughter, I'd certainly choose you. You are beautiful and I've always wanted a daughter. Thank you for coming to us!" and wrapped her in another big hug.

As Jeremiah ducked his head to enter the cabin, Caleb continued, "And Ma, you know how I've always been able to make just about any sound like the animals? Well, I've finally been stumped, course I only heard it once."

"Really? What was it?" she asked, taking the bait that she knew was being dangled before her.

"Well, there we were, me and Clancy, just stretchin' our legs and lookin' around for squirrels and there were none. But all of a sudden, through a clearing in the trees up yonder," he said pointing at an imaginary tree, "this big ol' bird came flyin' through them trees and it was squawkin' like nothin' I ever heard. Sounded like a cross between a buzzard and a bull-frog. Then it landed on its face in the dirt and didn't move. So me'n Clancy went runnin' over there thinkin' it was dead, and lo and behold, it was Pa!"

The cabin was filled with laughter that came from

tired travelers, a welcoming mother and wife, a proud Pa and a chuckling mountain man. As the laughter subsided, Jeremiah said, "Now cut that out! My ribs can't take it!"

"Well, if'n you had landed right, maybe that wouldn't be a problem now would it, ya ol' buzzard. Or was it bull-frog?" crowed Scratch, and the laughter began again.

While the elk-stew was hungrily consumed, the details of the trip and its many adventures were shared with Waters. She then inquired, "How bad was Shield wounded?"

"Aw, it wasn't too bad. It was already healin' up pretty good before we left. He'll be alright."

"And this woman warrior, Pine Leaf, will she live?"

"Yeah, I think so. Her wound was worse and it'll take more time. She also lost quite a bit of blood when she was hidin' in those bushes, but if she minds Shield I think she'll be O.K."

Waters then asked the same question women have been asking for generations, "Was she pretty?"

With a bit of a crooked smile and a glance at his wife, Jeremiah chuckled, "Oh, I spose, but not as pretty as you."

"Good answer," she replied. "What did Shield think of her?"

"Well, he was being pretty cautious, cuz she threat-ened to kill both of us! But to answer your real question, they were both kinda eyein' one another, so ya' never know. What with just the two of 'em up there, all alone an' all," he suggested with a mischievous smile. Jeremiah knew Waters was not jealous, but just concerned because Shield, Waters and White Wolf had all grown up together and were life-long friends. There had been several times that Waters had tried to put Shield together with some of her friends in hopes of making a couple, but had never succeeded.

After Jeremiah's meeting with Black Kettle, the word had been passed around the village that the move would begin in the morning and Jeremiah was anxious to get some rest before the journey began. Making Caleb share his loft space with his new sister and Scratch making a pallet of blankets on the floor near the fireplace, the newly expanded family turned in for the night in anticipation of the big move that would begin with the first light of morning.

WITH HER FEET DANGLING OVER THE EDGE OF THE loft, Clancy leaned back and looked at her new brother still asleep on his mat of blankets. Leaning forward to view the rest of the cabin, she looked at the still form of Scratch in front of the fireplace and its low-glowing embers still struggling to consume the stubs of wood at the far edges. The small tendril of smoke sought escape up the stone chimney while Clancy's eyes glazed over as her mind pondered all the changes in her life.

Just a few days, a couple of weeks really, ago she was a happy-go-lucky girl with a Mum and a Da that loved her and she spent her days happily running through the woods with her faithful companion, the big black dog Two Bits. Now she was in a remote cabin with strangers and with a whole village of Arapaho Indians camped just outside the door.

Yet she felt safe, maybe even a little bit happy, because she had a new family and a growing circle of friends. As she thought of Two Bits, she looked at his large bundle of fur stretched out beside Scratch. She knew Two Bits wasn't there when they all turned in for the night so he must have pushed his way through the door and made his bed beside the mountain man. He was almost as long as Scratch and easily larger in every other dimension. His chest rose and dropped in an even cadence and she could even hear his heavy breathing from where she sat.

As she watched, Scratch rolled over until he was face to face with Two Bits and the hot breath from the dog stirred him awake. Clancy muffled a giggle as she watched Scratch's eye pop wide open and his head jerk back as he yelled, "It's a bear, it's a bear right here in the house!"

His alarm startled Two Bits and he rose with a bark as he looked from Scratch to Clancy now giggling at the edge of the loft. Caleb sat up quickly, bumping his head on the low ceiling over his pallet of blankets and he shouted, "What's goin' on? What's wrong?"

Clancy couldn't answer as she leaned back laughing and pointed down to Scratch while she held her stomach. The bedroom door flew open and Jeremiah came quickly through wearing nothing but his red union suit and holding his pistol before him. He looked at Scratch then at Two Bits and laughed as Two Bits jumped up on his hind legs and started licking Scratch's face.

Looking at Jeremiah holding his pistol before him, Scratch said, "What were ya gonna do with that pop-gun against a bear?" Jeremiah responded with a droll expression, "Wal, I figgered it'd make him made'nuff to start chewin' on you and we could escape! Course, bout the time he got a good taste of your on'ry hide he'd run outta here on his own!"

Waters peeked around Jeremiah and started laughing as she said, "Scratch, you're supposed to protect us from those big bear, not play licky-face with them!"

Scratch grumbled his only response as he rubbed the big dog behind his ears and pushed him back down on all fours. Scratch went to the slightly ajar door and let the dog out to explore the area.

The scraggly faced man turned back to Jeremiah and asked, "Well, ya just gonna stand there in yore unner-wares or are ya gonna get dressed so we can get this here outfit on the way?" he questioned in an attempt to get the attention off his early morning false alarm. Jeremiah turned back into his bedroom and shut the door for a bit of privacy while he and Waters readied themselves for the coming day.

Clancy turned and let herself down from the loft without using the nearby ladder as she simply dropped to the length of her arms and then let go to drop lightly to the floor. She started preparations for the morning meal by stirring up the embers and adding several pieces of wood for the morning cook fire.

The pot of left-overs from the night before hung on the swinging arm at the side of the opening and Clancy removed the lid to examine the contents. Grabbing a spoon hanging nearby, she stirred up the remains of the elk stew. She easily found her way around the goods on the nearby counter and started mixing up some corn meal and other fixings for some corn bread biscuits to go with the remaining elk stew.

By the time Jeremiah and Waters came from the bedroom, the biscuits were cooking and the stew was heating and all would soon be ready for the morning meal. Caleb and Scratch had already left the cabin for their morning constitutional and now returned to the cabin and seated themselves at the rough-hewn split log table. Turning to Jeremiah, Scratch said, "So how long ya think it'll take all these folks to get ready to hit the trail?"

Jeremiah chuckled and answered, "They'll probably be ready 'fore we are, they're purty experienced at packin' up and movin' out on short notice. And they've been waitin' for the word to move for some time now, so what with they're bein' anxious an' all, we'll probably be movin' out around mid-day or before."

"Ya think so? That's a purty big bunch o' folks out there an' it looks like more'n half of 'em are wimmen an' I ain't never know wimmen ta' git in a hurry 'bout nuthin'!"

"And just how many 'wimmin' have you knowd?" Jeremiah asked knowing that Scratch's experience with the fairer sex was somewhat limited.

Waters spoke up and said, "You know there are two of us 'wimmin' right here listening to you make those comments about us, and we haven't served you breakfast yet," with an impudent expression on her face that made her look insulted.

"Well, you know, present company excepted . . .uh you understand, don'tcha? Mebbe I just better shut up," mumbled Scratch as he tucked his chin toward his chest as he looked down at the floor.

"Ummhummm. . ." responded Waters laughing.

The light mood continued throughout the camp as

everyone busily prepared for the coming journey. It was good to have something to look forward to and everyone eagerly anticipated the new camp away from the blackened memories of the past. Lodges soon fell to the busy hands of the women and packs were prepared by the remaining family members. Horses were brought into the clearing and packs were assembled or made to handle the many parfleche of the people.

Some were stuffed with personal belongings, some with smoked meats and pemmican, while others carried a variety of essential items including weapons and gear. There were still a few injured that would not be able to walk and travois were prepared for them. The larger lodges or teepees also required a travois for transport. The brush huts consisted of bent saplings and other branches and covered by hides or tarpaulins were disassembled and only the essential elements were prepared for the trip.

Jeremiah's two pack mules were used for packing the remaining stores of meat and the fresh kill of buffalo that had been stored in the cavern. The mules were sturdier and the packs better suited for the heavier loads. They would use two additional horses and their own horses to pack the remainder of goods they would take with them for this winter move. Jeremiah's prophecy of a mid-day departure was fulfilled as he took the lead of the large cavalcade and started down the trail that would lead them to the Wind River valley.

As the trail dropped off the shoulder of the last of the foothills, its width permitted Black Kettle to move to the side of Jeremiah. Scratch and Caleb were scouting the trail a couple of miles distant in front of the slow moving village. As the leader of the Arapaho joined Jeremiah he asked, "White Wolf, tell me more about the Crow and the Blackfeet you fought with your brother Broken Shield."

Jeremiah began to relate all the events leading up to the battle and all the details about the attack of the Black-feet and the terrible toll of the dead among both tribes. With an explanation of the wounds of both Shield and Pine Leaf, he also detailed the actions taken to provide a safe haven for the two wounded warriors. All the while Jeremiah spoke, Black Kettle listened attentively as both men rocked to the gait of their mounts on the rough trail.

Occasionally he would ask a question to clarify some action or decision and with a grunt or a wave of his hand he would signal White Wolf to continue his narration. Although both men were immersed in the conversation, they continued their close observation of the terrain around them for any sign of danger or alarm. When Jere-miah concluded his account of the previous week's happenings, he noticed Scratch and Caleb waiting to the side of the trail. When he and Black Kettle neared the waiting scouts, they stopped to listen to Scratch's report.

"We're about an hour or so from a likely campin' spot up yonder. There's a bit of a stream coming down through that small gorge and it'll probly be 'nuff for ever-body," then he paused but Jeremiah knew there was more the mountain man was concerned about. "And . . .?" Jere-miah asked.

"And what with all the dust ya'll are raisin' even a blind man can see ya' comin', it might be a purty good idée if we traveled at night or real early in the mornin' if ya' don't want nobody ta' see ya, that is," and he nodded back down the trail to point out the rising cloud of dust. The long drought and the already dry trails made every footfall stir up small clouds of powdery dust and with as many on the trail as were traveling, a large dust cloud naturally followed. The absence of any breeze to move the dust clouds made it impossible for this number of travelers to move undetected. Black Kettle and Jeremiah turned to observe what they already knew they would see, a large wispy cloud of dust rising over the tops of the scattered pines and pinions of the foothills.

As they approached the campsite, the many travelers scattered out to claim their individual portion of the camp. They were like a well-organized army as the youngsters disappeared into the nearby trees to gather firewood, the women began preparing the fires and the men took care of the horses. Within a short while the families were gathered by their fires anticipating the evening meal. The fires were small and smokeless as the youngsters knew that dead and dried wood gave off little smoke and the necessity for going undetected was great. After the meal, Black Kettle and two of the other leaders strolled to the camp of Jeremiah and Waters. She offered coffee to her visitors but was refused as the men settled themselves to the ground near the fire.

Black Kettle, Mankiller, and Walking Bear were the leaders of the village, and all were proven warriors. Yet the circle of leaders was missing two others that would normally have been with them for any type of council, but they were victims of the fire. One, Horsecatcher, still lived but was unable to walk as he continued to recover from his massive burns. Black Kettle spoke, "We have talked about the counsel of your friend, Scratch. When he says we should travel at night to keep from showing our presence. His counsel is good, but we have chosen to travel during the day. We will not crawl into our winter quarters."

Jeremiah started to speak but was stopped by the upraised hand of Black Kettle. He continued, "We will have Badger and Raven scout the distant valley beside our people. Scratch will continue to scout the far trail before us. If we do not go boldly, and the Crow see us, they will think we are afraid. We are not!"

Jeremiah looked at Scratch and turned back to Black Kettle and the other leaders. He carefully considered his words before he spoke, "You are wise in your words and your choice. I agree with you my Uncle, and we will do as you say. I also believe the Crow, if they are around, it will only be to find the remains of their warriors that were lost in the battle with the Blackfeet. I think the number of their warriors is less and they will not be looking for a fight."

Black Kettle nodded his head in agreement and turned to see Laughing Waters seated behind Jeremiah and said, "Now, my daughter, we will have the coffee you offered. Do you have sugar?" he asked smiling. As Laughing Waters rose to her feet to do her father's bidding, she replied, "Yes, my father, I know you want lots of sugar and we have some for you." The other leaders nodded their heads in agreement and indicated their desire for the sweet addition to their cups.

Scratch started to rise and said to Jeremiah, "Well, if

we're gonna get some sleep, I better get some guards posted. You can take the first watch and I'll get a couple others and I'll take the last watch in the early mornin' so's I can get out on the trail early. I'll probly take the young'un with me, if that's O.K.?" Jeremiah nodded his assent to his friend and turned to continue the visit with his father-in-law, Black Kettle.

BLACK BADGER AND RAVEN'S WING WERE THE SONS of Buffalo Thunder and Walking Dove. Buffalo Thunder was Jeremiah's adopted father and mentor known as Ezekiel. Both had proven themselves as warriors and were often chosen for special tasks. Although in their teens, the young men resembled their father in stature and manner. Badger was the larger of the two and his frame was beginning to fill out as his fathers, while Raven reflected the leaner appearance of his mother.

Both would probably approach six feet when they reached their mature growth and while Badger would easily top two hundred pounds, the lean frame of Raven would be more suited for speed and stealth rather than bulk and brawn like his brother. Two years separated them with Raven being the younger, but their skill with weapons and hunting and in battle had earned the respect of the warrior society which was not determined by age.

While the caravan of the village held near the tree

line by the foothills, the scouts dropped farther into the valley toward the river basin with about two miles separating them from the people. The Wind River was about fifteen miles to the northeast but there were ample streams coming from the mountains that shadowed them. Scratch and Caleb were about two miles farther up the trail on their scout as the village started their trek toward their winter camp. They expected to be another two to four days on the trail depending on how the many members of the village were able to travel. There were still several injured, some on travois that made the progress slower than hoped.

Clancy Mae and Laughing Waters rode side by side and continued their 'getting acquainted' conversation of the previous day. They were both enjoying the time together as Waters shared, "My father, Black Kettle, is the shaman or medicine man of the village as well as one of the elders or members of the leadership council. It is our tradition that the leader of the family or the elder member of the family is the one that gives the names and spirit tokens to the new members of the family." She paused before resuming, "And he has given you a name," she smiled as she looked at Clancy.

The girl turned a questioning look to Waters and asked, "What is it? Is it a good one? Tell me." She pleaded.

"Sun of The Morning. It is because of the color of your hair. My father and most of the people of our village have never seen anyone with hair the color of yours. He thinks it is a special blessing from the Creator and reminds him of the colors that paint the sky in the early morning."

"Sun of The Morning," she repeated and sat a little straighter in her saddle and put her shoulders back. Lifting a hand to her hair and brushing it away from her ears, she turned to Waters and said, "That's kinda pretty. I like it."

Waters smiled at her new daughter and agreed, "Yes, I think so too. But with each name comes the responsibility to make sure that you do nothing to dishonor the name. If you dishonor it, it also dishonors he who gave it to you."

Clancy giggled, "That means that Caleb is your son, and I'm your Sun of the Morning!"

Waters laughed and smiled as the two shared a special moment. Clancy asked, "Does that mean that your father, Black Kettle, will also name your new baby?"

"Yes, he will. But our children don't receive their names from the elder until they have lived some years and shown what they should be named. Until then we usually have baby names or children names like mouse or chipmunk or something that we use until they receive their real names."

Changing the subject, Clancy asked, "Will you teach me to use the bow and arrow? Caleb said you were the best with the bow in the entire village. I would really like to learn how."

"Yes, I will. I also brought a bow I used when I was younger, just so you would have one to use. And I will teach you how to make arrows and all the many other things you will need to know as you grow to womanhood," declared Waters.

Clancy's smile spread across her face with a flash of

white teeth that showed her surprise and pleasure, then said, "I could hug you right now, I'm so happy!"

Waters leaned from her saddle and wrapped an arm around her daughter and gave her a big hug that told the girl she was loved. As they continued on the trail, both fell silent as they contemplated the goodness and joy that each would bring the other. Clancy couldn't help comparing Waters with her mother and knew they were nearing the place where her mother and father were killed by the raiding Crow.

A combination of joy and sadness seemed to wrap its arms around the girl and she was confused. *Am I wrong to love Waters? Am I doing wrong by my Mum if I love Waters? If I could talk to my Mum, I wonder if she would be upset with me for loving Waters? And what would she think about my new Indian name? Maybe she would be glad I found a family. Yeah, I think she would be, maybe it's all right then.*

Badger and Raven traveled together as they ventured farther into the valley for their scout. The rolling terrain was dotted by patches of sagebrush and buffalo grass that did little to disguise their presence. By keeping to the lower areas between the small hillocks, they would not be easily seen, but their vision was also hindered. Knowing any threat would come from the northeast side of the valley, they kept out of sight whenever possible but would carefully approach any crest of a hill and view the area before revealing themselves.

As Raven neared the top of one of the larger rises, he peered over the top between two large clumps of sage. Within twenty yards, four antelopes were lazily grazing on the few clumps of brown grass. Without moving, he scanned the valley and far-off tree line for any sign of danger and seeing none, he backed down from the crest. Motioning his brother, he drew an arrow from his quiver and awaited his brother.

"Four antelope... our people could use the meat. One bigger buck and three does, the doe are to the left. You take the far one and I'll take the one in the middle," he whispered. With a nod of his head, he signaled his brother and together they rose from behind the sage. Swiftly drawing their bows to the full length of the arrows, they let fly together and sent the flint tipped arrows to their chosen targets.

Their surprise was complete and both doe jumped and fell to the ground. While Raven retrieved their mounts, Badger started field dressing the animals. Making short work of their task, the brothers draped the animals across the rumps of their horses and mounted up to return to the trail and the travelers. When they crossed the trail, it was evident the villagers had yet to pass so they hung the carcasses from a nearby tree where they would be seen and retrieved by the people. Returning to their scouting duties, the brothers trotted their mounts across the valley floor towards the river.

A streambed lined with a cluster of cottonwood afforded sufficient cover for the two scouts and the men dropped from their horses for a mid-day meal. A small fire at the edge of the little trickle of a stream licked at the strips of antelope liver that hung suspended on green willow branches. Raven tended the meat while Badger stood on the bank next to a grey snag of a dead cottonwood that was now devoid of its bark. Careful to not provide a silhouette, Badger scanned the far away banks of the Wind River. There was nothing moving anywhere within his eyesight, either by the river or on the undulating hills of the valley. He turned and dropped down the bank to join his brother for the meal.

Conversation was not always necessary for the two brothers, they were like many close siblings and understood both thoughts and intents of each other with little being said between them. Like most young men their thoughts were usually occupied by the girls of their village. They both often expressed the desire to travel to other villages of the people to look for a mate. It was a common practice for the villages to come together for celebrations and socializing but this year had been different. The drought and the fire had made that travel of lesser importance than the getting of game and preparing for the winter.

"I was thinking about going to the village of Standing Elk after we get to our winter camp," stated Badger. Both brothers knew they would have to help their mother get settled into the new camp and have her winter supply laid in before they could consider leaving. Raven looked as his brother and replied, "You are thinking about Little Bird," and smiled.

"And you haven't been thinking about Flower in the Mist?" kidded Badger, knowing his brother was just as enamored with Mist as he was with Bird. The two girls were sisters and the daughters of the village leader, Standing Elk. They met the girls three years before and had anxiously anticipated seeing them again this year, but the fire had changed the plans of the village and now the young men were conspiring ways to see the girls again.

"They might already be taken," said Raven a bit fearfully.

"No, she promised she would wait," firmly stated Badger, thinking of Little Bird and their last time together. Their friendship had grown rapidly and whenever the villages were together, Bird and Badger were inseparable. Both families knew of the many times the two would 'accidently' be in the same place at the same time, but the way of young people was known and appreciated by all.

Raven and Mist had become close because of the many times they assisted their siblings in their rendezvous. Now, both couples were thinking about their futures together and making a family. Tradition would have the men to join the village of the women because the lodges were always considered to belong to the women. Men were allowed only when invited and if the couple were considered married and the woman wanted to end it, she would simply put his belongings outside of the lodge and they were no longer a couple. Yet, even with these considerations, both brothers were anxious to see the sisters again, and the sooner the better.

"It will be at least one moon and maybe two before we can leave and by then the snows might soon come," stated Raven.

"If it does, we might have to spend the winter with Standing Elks band," grinned Badger.

Chuckling together, the two brothers mounted up

and returned to the scouting task for the village. The remainder of the day was uneventful and they soon returned to join the village for the night's camp. Tomorrow would bring them to the edge of the river as the mountain valley narrowed near the headwaters of the Wind River. When they neared the river, the route to the winter camp would take them across the floor of the valley before they would find cover among the trees again.

As the line of sunlight crawled from treetop to treetop down the eastern slope of the opposite mountain, Broken Shield put his hands behind his head and watched as the new day made itself known. Pushing the shadows before it, the light of the dawn finally reached the tree-line on its quest toward the valley floor.

This was the third day since the battle and Shield thought his wound was healing nicely. There would be soreness and weakness in his shoulder for some time to come, but he was rapidly regaining full use of his arm. He turned to look at Pine Leaf lying in the shelter still wrapped in the lazy arms of slumber. Her wound, though more extensive than Shield's, was also healing well. She had lost more blood and the weakness from such a wound would be her companion for several days. The red meat from the deer would replenish her blood, but time was the necessary element for proper healing.

Her eyes opened and she saw Shield looking at her but she was no longer alarmed when the big Arapaho watched her, he had been her caretaker for several days and had shown himself to be a friend. "Are you going to fix us something to eat, or do you expect me to do it?" she asked sarcastically.

Their communication had become a mix of Arapaho and Crow with sign language bridging the gaps, but both were comfortable with their understanding. While it was common for the many different peoples to learn the language of others, neither Shield nor Leaf were fluent in both languages. Yet the necessity of clear understanding brought both to the common ground of the mixed languages.

He laughed at her question and responded, "I don't think a pipe bearer nor a war leader would know much about making food that would be good to eat. Until you are better, I will make the meals so we will both get better and not die from eating bad food."

She grunted a response, but a smile tugged at the corners of her mouth that she could not contain and her amusement was evident. "You will make someone a good wife," she responded chuckling with laughter.

With a grunt of protest, he lifted himself erect and went to the fire to stir the embers to life. With the fire going, he went the remaining quarter of the deer that hung suspended from the nearby ponderosa and sliced off a couple of thin steaks for the two of them. After skewering them onto the green willow branches, he hung the meat over the fire. From his diminishing supply he grabbed a handful of coffee beans and started grinding them on the nearby flat stone to make their morning coffee.

A trill of a low whistle from Leaf caught his attention and turning to her, he saw her motion to the lower valley. Three mounted warriors were crossing the creek at the lower end of the valley with their attention focused on the ground searching for sign of any other intruders to the high mountain meadow. They were painted for war and with weapons in hand, Shield identified them as Blackfeet, probably scouts on the hunt for the larger party that had not returned.

When the warrior in the lead motioned to the ground, then turned to scan the upper reaches of the valley, Shield knew they had seen sign that would give away their presence. Quickly he rose to a low crouch and returned to his blankets where his bow and quiver lay alongside his rifle. Looking at Leaf, he watched as she struggled to her feet and reached for her bow, quiver and knife. With hand signals, he motioned her to a cluster of fir and spruce saplings with chokecherries at their base indicating she was to wait there at the ready. He then motioned that he would circle below their location to ambush the warriors if they were to come to their camp.

The Blackfeet spread out and started on a direct path toward the camp of Shield and Leaf. Shield knelt behind a cluster of kinnikinnick and scrub oak near a thick copse of spruce. He was slightly below the camp and on the downhill side but was well obscured from sight. As they neared the tree-line, the warriors dropped from their mounts, tying them off to a nearby shrub and with arrows nocked, they started their stealthy approach.

It was evident to them from the smell of smoke and cooking meat they were close so their approach was slow but deliberate. Shield watched and was impressed with their ability to move silently through the thicker underbrush and many pine saplings. As they approached the clearing, they could tell no one was present, but the sizzling steaks over the fire betrayed their nearness. The three warriors dropped to a crouching stance as they surveyed the area for any sign of their quarry.

Leaf and Shield remained motionless and silent. Shield was confident that Leaf would not betray her presence as the patience of the attackers soon wore thin. With nodded agreement, the three rose and quickly entered the camp but turned with their backs to the center to watch for any attack from without the circle. With none forthcoming, their tense stance relaxed and they released the draw on their bows as they started to turn to each other, Shield let fly with the first well aimed arrow that sped silently on its assigned course to penetrate the back of the apparent leader of the group.

His only warning of attack was when he looked down to see four inches of arrow shaft with the jagged edged arrow head protruding from his chest. His last word was nothing more than a grunt as his knees buckled and he dropped face forward into the fire. Another arrow from the uphill hideaway of Leaf sped toward the second warrior but the weakened Leaf was unable to have a full draw on her bow and the arrow fell short of its target and pierced the thigh of the warrior that screamed in alarm and pain.

Shield had dropped his bow and charged at the remaining warrior as he started to raise his bow at the now visible and charging target. Yet before he could draw back the arrow, the tomahawk in Shield's hand sunk into the side of the warrior's head and split his ear as it shattered the skull. The embedded tomahawk was jerked from Shield's hand as the warrior dropped at his feet and Shield faced the remaining warrior that now turned to meet the new threat.

Ignoring the arrow in his thigh, he dropped his bow and snatched his knife from the scabbard at his waist. Dropping into a crouch and emitting a snarl like a cornered wolf, the warrior readied himself for Shield's attack. Shield also drew his knife and began to circle the wounded Blackfoot, knowing it would be difficult for the man to continue to move on the wounded leg. A quick glance at the man's wound showed pulsing blood pouring from around the arrow, but the man reached down and broke off the arrow and screamed as he tried to charge the Arapaho.

Shield quickly stepped aside and pushed the man as he fell forward. Catching himself with a grimace on his face, the man turned to face Shield again. With a feint to the left, Shield moved to protect himself, and the warrior lunged with his arm fully extended and sliced the side of Shield as he fell forward.

While the Blackfoot staggered to catch himself, Shield whirled around behind him, grabbed his hair and jerked his head up and with a swift move, Shield sliced open the warrior's throat and almost decapitated him. Dropping the now dead man at his feet, Shield turned to see Leaf moving swiftly to his side. She put her shoulder under his arm and helped him to his blankets, opened his tunic and looked at the wound. Although bleeding freely, it was not deep and she knew a poultice and bandage would be sufficient for the wound.

With just a few minutes to recoup his breath, a stench spread from the fire as the hair of the second warrior flared from the flames. Burning flesh caused both Shield and Leaf to make faces of disgust and they joined efforts to drag the dead Blackfoot from the fire.

"I must move the horses and wipe out their sign. We don't know if there are others and we must not be found again," mulled Shield as he looked at Leaf. She was breathing heavily and the color had drained from her face revealing her still weakened condition.

"We can use the horses to move the bodies. There is a rock outcropping back there a short way that we can use to bury them. But I think we should eat first because we need the strength," she replied.

Shield nodded his agreement and motioned her to return to her bedroll within the shelter and he would bring the food. It was only a few paces back to her blankets, but he noticed her struggle and weakness as she dropped to her bedroll and turned to await him. He brought a cup of coffee, the strip steak and the camas root that he roasted in the coals. She was surprised at the sweet treat of the Camas but was pleased with his efforts to provide a good meal.

They ate quietly as each retreated into their own thoughts as to the start of the day and what the day might yet hold for them. Shield finished his meal, downed the last of his coffee and stood to start the task before him. "You stay here and rest, it is not a hard job before me and I will do it quickly. I will use their horses to leave a trail away from here and then return to wipe out their trail. When I am done, I will return and remove the bodies."

"Let me fix your side first. We need to stop the bleeding," she reminded him. He went to the packs and obtained the medicinal plants for a poultice. He ground the chickweed and Hound's Tongue leaves together in his palm, letting the dried remains drop onto the flat rock by the fire, then putting the flaky particles into the remains of the coffee, he made a paste in his palm then went to Leaf. He allowed her to use a patch of buckskin and some strips to secure the poultice to his side. He stood and looking down at her, he motioned for her to rest and he would soon return.

Backtracking the Blackfoot ponies, the path took him to the same trail he and Jeremiah used when they scouted the valley. Once again he used a handful of branches from the scrub oak to wipe clear the tracks leading to the upper trail. Leading two horses and riding the third, he moved further down the trail to where the tracks intermingled with the tracks of the Crow when they were led into the ambush.

Finding a break in the brush, he dropped from his mount and led the animals off the trail toward the higher meadow, and returned to the path to once again obscure his tracks. He returned to their camp and began the task of dragging the bodies of the warrior Blackfeet to the rocky outcropping where he would climb up and push off enough of the rocks to bury the bodies. It was tiring work and the effort to move the stones took the remainder of his strength. He sat down at the base of a tall pine and rested before taking the Blackfoot ponies to the clearing where his two horses were tethered. His mount was glad to see him and after taking a few moments to rub his forehead and pat his neck, speaking softly to him all the while, Shield finally turned to make his way back to camp.

He was tired and perhaps a little less cautious than normal, although after the early morning attack, he should have been more vigilant. Perhaps it was his thoughts about Leaf that garnered his attention, he had been thinking about her a lot, or perhaps it was his anticipation of the arrival of his people, but he was not as observant as he should have been. Approaching the camp, his head was down as he walked into the clearing. Standing before him were five Crow warriors, each with a bow at full draw and holding a nocked arrow aimed at his chest.

Scratch and Caleb marked the trail well and now as dusk was fast approaching, Jeremiah and Black Kettle led the moving village out of the tree-line and across the sage clustered slope to the cottonwood and alder lined bank of the Wind River. Across the water Scratch and Caleb sat astride their mounts and waved at the approaching leaders of the cavalcade. The crossing chosen by the mountain man was downstream from the site of the wagon train massacre survived by Clancy Mae and appeared to be shallow and with a stone littered bottom.

A sudden scream of a war cry caught the attention of White Wolf and Black Kettle as they reined their horses to their right to try to spot the source. Across the river and some three hundred yards away but coming fast were Badger and Raven, screaming their warning to those about to cross. Another couple hundred yards behind them came four or five pursuing warriors screaming and waving their war clubs in the air. Lying along the necks of their mounts, the two Arapaho scouts were whipping their horses with short quirts to get top speed from them while they shouted encouragement into the horses' ears.

Jeremiah spurred his mount across the stream and was followed closely by Black Kettle with other warriors kicking up dust with their eager mounts in pursuit of their leaders. Scratch and Caleb had turned their horses to face the oncoming threat and both slid from their saddles to take a knee with a stable elbow to knee stance for a steady shot if needed. Jeremiah and Kettle slid to a stop beside the two but remained on their horses, turning them to face the charge. Three other Arapaho warriors joined them and formed a line almost shoulder to shoulder beside Jeremiah. With Scratch and Caleb before them, the gathered men presented a formidable front as Badger and Raven skidded to a stop at the end of the line. The threat of the additional number of Arapaho had not slowed the rampaging charge of the screaming attackers, that were stirred on by the increasing adrenaline and promise of glory in battle.

"They are stupid young'uns that are bent on bringin' blood when it ain't necessary. Scratch, drop that lead one's horse! Caleb, take aim on the next one but hold your fire!"

Before Jeremiah finished his orders, Scratch touched off his shot. The thunderous roar echoed back from the mountainside behind them as the smoke pole made the presence of the death-dealer known. The horse did a flip as certain as if its front legs dropped in a gopher hole and its rider flew twenty yards through the air, landing in front of the other attackers that had to veer their horses to the side to keep from trampling him to death. That move caused the others to focus on their leader as they circled their mounts beside their fallen comrade.

One reached down and helped his friend as he swung up behind his helper. It was evident the small group was arguing heatedly, but reason finally prevailed and they turned their backs on their previously intended quarry. Two of the retreating warriors turned and waved their war clubs as they shouted threats to the Arapaho and were answered in kind by those alongside Jeremiah. As Jeremiah looked at Kettle, both men smiled knowingly and remembered their own youthful times of taunting others.

Black Kettle went to Badger and Raven to question them on their scout while Jeremiah conferred with Scratch. They agreed the evening's camp should be here beside the river and the morrow would be the last day of their trek allowing ample time to reach the site of their winter camp. Scratch remounted while he was talking with Jeremiah and the conversation continued with Jeremiah pointing across the sage covered valley to the broad green expanse between the two mountain ranges on the North side of the Wind River valley they now occupied. "You can reach the trail up to that valley over yonder at the base of that mountain over there. It's a purty good trail but that's a climb for sure. Caleb's been there n' he can help ya find it, mebbe save ya' some time."

"Judgin' by the colors, looks like thar's a purty good bunch of scrub oak an' stuff there," Scratch observed.

"Yeah, but the trail parts the way purty good, but it's

also a good hidin' place, so keep yore eyes open, as ya allus do."

The men turned their attention to helping the rest of the villagers to the camp site. Those that were carried in Travois in need of help getting across the stream. Two mounted men would pick up the ends of the travois and the third would lead the horse bearing the wounded across the stream to deposit it on the other side. Several travois, some bearing wounded and some with lodge covers or other baggage, would need assistance to cross to keep the occupants above water. Most of the injured were mending well, but the more severely burned would be months in healing. Constant care from family members and the Shaman would ensure a good recovery, but until then, the entire village assisted each one.

As usual, the experienced villagers made short work of the camp set-up and the evening meal was soon sizzling over the flames or coals of the cook fires. Waters and Clancy, or Sun of the Morning, made a good team and the meal for the rest of the extended family was soon ready for the hungry scouts and leader of the trek. Jeremiah was the first to reach for a juicy steak, but received a slap from a long forked stick in the hand of Waters. "Don't get in such a hurry, you know I will serve you when it's ready!" she admonished, smiling at her husband.

"Woman, I'm hungry and I don't cotton to gettin' slapped with a stick. Am I gonna have to take you over my knee?" he threatened.

Waters stood, stretched her tunic tight across her enlarged belly now showing her pregnancy more than before, and said, "I'd just roll off!" she smiled mischievously. "Now just sit down and I'll get your food."

It was the custom among most Native peoples for the men to eat their fill first and the wives and children to wait until the men were finished. However, Jeremiah had never been a stickler for that particular custom and preferred to eat with his family. As Waters handed him a carved wood bowl, he leaned back against the trunk of the fallen cottonwood and waited for her to join him.

She motioned the others to help themselves as she seated herself beside her husband. When all had their portions, Jeremiah, according to a custom he had initiated, asked the blessing of God on his family and gave thanks for the provision of the meal and the safety for the day. As he concluded with an "Amen" everyone began consuming the delicious buffalo stew prepared by the women.

After the meal, the extended family was seated around the fire and enjoying the time together as Jeremiah tossed the well-worn Bible to Caleb and said, "Don't ya think ya oughta catch up on some of your reading son?"

True to form of any teen-ager, Caleb groaned but replied, "Yeah, I spose," and began flipping pages to the assigned location. Clancy scooted over next to Caleb to read over his shoulder and to make sure Caleb was getting it right. He began, "Verse 6, 'Be careful for nothing; but in everything by prayer and suppli, uh, suppli ca tion, What's that mean Pa," he asked.

"Well, supplication is real strong askin', you know, when you really want something and you get real anxious about it, you ask real serious like, understand?" answered Jeremiah.

"Okay, " and he continued, ". . . supplication with thanksgiving, let your requests be made known unto God. Verse 7, And the peace of God, which passeth understanding, shall keep your hearts and minds through Christ Jesus." As he finished, he furrowed his brow and looked at his dad and asked, "Does that mean we're supposed to take everything to Him in prayer, and He'll give us peace about it, even though we don't understand it?"

"That's very good, son. That's exactly what it means. No matter what troubles us, if we take it to the Lord in prayer, we can leave it with Him and He'll give us peace about it, both in our hearts and minds."

Clancy chimed in, "You mean, no matter what we're thinkin' or feelin' if we pray about it, He'll take care of it?" but she had a doubtful look on her face.

"Well, not always the way we think it should be, Clancy, but no matter what happens, whether we agree with it or not, if we trust Him," he said pointing to the Heavens, "He will give us peace about it and the strength to accept His will."

He knew she was thinking about the deaths of her parents and the others. It had been a burden hard to bear for a young girl and a confusing one to try to understand. He allowed her to digest the truth of his words and didn't push her for a response.

"What about this, 'Be careful for nothing' part? I thought we were supposed to be careful about everything?" asked Caleb.

Scratch joined in with, "That just means don't worry 'bout nothin' cuz worryin' don't do ya no good."

"Whatcha mean, Uncle Scratch?"

"Well, lemme see hyar. Did your momma back in Michigan have a rockin' chair?" he asked the boy.

"Yeah, it was her favorite chair. She'd sit in it by the fireplace and do her knittin'" he fondly remembered.

"Did she rock in it? You know, back 'n forth 'n such?"

"Yeah, all the time, every stitch she took, she'd rock away," he smiled as he thought about it.

"Did she get anywhere? Ya know, anywhere besides there at the fireplace?"

Caleb laughed and replied, "No, of course not. Ya don't get anywhere in a rockin' chair."

"Same with worryin' it don't getcha anywhere either. 'stead o' worryin' 'bout sumpin' your 'sposed to pray about it and leave it with the Lord."

Caleb looked at his Uncle Scratch and tilting his head like Two Bits he pondered the statement. He looked at the big dog, then at Clancy who was also pondering what had been said, then turned back to Scratch and asked, "Do you do that? Pray, I mean, and leave it with the Lord?"

"Yup, shore do, all the time," he firmly stated, then spit a stream of tobacco juice into the flames and listened to it sizzle.

A pensive mood settled on the family as they all stared into the fire and lost themselves in their own thoughts and silent prayers.

THE TOWERING GRANITE CRAGS OF THE ABSAROKA Mountain Range were a welcome sight to the villagers. The sentinel peaks that seemed to scratch the blue of the sky signaled the travelers their destination was near. Word had already spread as to the location of their winter camp and those that had traveled this part of the country well knew of the rich valleys of the Absaroka.

The view of the mountains was accented by the afternoon sun that shone from a cloudless sky as a welcome to the weary that longed for their new home. The long line of travelers snaked its way through the thick brush that covered the lower slopes leading to the high mountain valley. Now as it stretched out, the line was filled with eager faces and animated conversations among the many members of the village.

Scratch and Caleb were joined by Clancy Mae early that morning and the three crossed the Shoshone Creek that would later become known as the South Fork of the Shoshone River. As their horses broke through the willows along the north bank, Scratch held up his hand in a signal to stop and be silent. The two youngsters that had been talking non-stop all morning, now quickly fell silent as they pulled their horses to the side of the trail and obscured themselves in the tall willows. Scratch slowly backed his horse alongside the two and whispered, "There's a whole herd of elk out yonder. They's a ways off, but I don't wanna scare 'em, so let's go back to Jeremiah an' see if'n they wanna get some fresh meat."

Watching the three riders returning toward him, Jeremiah was both surprised and alarmed. When Scratch stopped on a slight shoulder of hillside that was bare of the thick brush, he waited for his friend to join him and the youngsters. Black Kettle and Jeremiah reined up beside the smiling scouts and Jeremiah asked, "I can tell by your faces it ain't nuthin' dangerous, so what is it that's got you all smilin' so big?"

"Boy, it's the dangest sight ya ever did see. I only seen it onct before myself."

"All right, c'mon, what's got everybody so excited?" asked Jeremiah again.

"Thar's a herd o' elk up thar in that big ol' meadow, and they's all bulls! About thirty or so of 'em, every one is a bull, like it's some kinda gatherin' for the boys or sompin'," then turning to Black Kettle he asked, "Have you ever seen that before? Nuthin' but bulls all gathered up together?"

"Yes. Sometimes in late summer before the rut begins and they start fighting, the bulls gather together, but it is not often seen. This is a good sign. We will make meat."

He turned and waved several of his men forward to begin to plan the hunt.

With Jeremiah, Scratch and Caleb joining in the planning with Black Kettle and six chosen warriors, the strategy was soon settled. Then Scratch said, "Jeremiah, you ain't gonna be no good with yore busted wing in a sling, so mebbe you oughta let Clancy or Waters take yore Hawken to help with the hunt."

"I can still shoot," he argued with a scowl on his face.

"Yeah, mebbe if somebody holds your weapon for ya," Scratch said, "But if somebody's gotta hold it, and reload it, you might as well just let them shoot it too!"

Waters was now beside her husband and as she looked at him, she motioned for him to let Clancy take his rifle and said, "You said she was a good shot and got that antelope, so she should be able to get an elk, after all, they are a bigger target." Then smiling at her husband, she reached down and pulled his Hawken from its scabbard and laid it across her legs, motioning for Clancy to come and get it and the powder horn and possibles bag now hanging on Jeremiah's extended good arm. Clancy had a broad smile and a twinkle in her eyes as she draped the possibles bag and powder horn over her head and shoulder and reached for the rifle. Feeling like she was a mighty hunter, she proudly joined Scratch and Caleb.

Jeremiah looked at Waters then at the departing hunters and back to Waters and said, "It's almost like we got three kids and they're all growed up and leavin' home, makes me feel old, like an old grandpa and I ain't even thirty years old." He stated then followed with, "At least I don't think I'm thirty yet, am I?" Waters laughed and smiled at her befuddled husband.

The strategy was for all the hunters to move into the trees on the east side of the valley to make their way closer to the herd of elk. Then those with rifles, Scratch, Talks With the Wind, Sun of the Morning, and Black Kettle, to drop down into the valley as surreptitiously as possible while the others worked their way above the herd. At the predetermined signal to be given by the leader of the larger group led by Raven Walking, the rifles would take their shots. When the elk spooked and ran away from the shooters, the remainder of the hunters would then descend on them and take as many as possible.

Kettle led the hunters as they worked their way through the thick timber along the lower portion of the West face of the Absaroka. Moving as silently as possible, it took almost an hour for the ten hunters to reach the point of separation. As Kettle and the other rifle bearers slid from their mounts, Raven Walking and Black Badger led the others further into the timber toward their destination. Tethering their mounts in the trees, Scratch and Kettle with Caleb and Clancy following walked in a hunched over manner to let the tall grasses and scattered shrubs shield them from the view of the elk.

Moving slowly, the four reached a thicket of scrub oak that stretched above their heads and they dropped to their knees to select their positions for the hunt. Kettle took the point farthest to the left and Scratch the point farthest to the right, leaving the two youngsters in the middle and with an advantageous position behind a sizable cluster of boulders that seemed out of place in the midst of the grassy meadow.

"You take that side and use the edge of the boulder for a rest," whispered Caleb, "but make sure the end of the barrel is away from any points of rock or anything. Sometimes you can see through the sights, but a rock can kinda stick up just in front of the barrel and cause a ricochet."

Clancy looked at him in wonder, then looked at the boulder and saw the irregularity of the shape and realized what he said was possible. She lay the rifle on the boulder and pulled it back to her shoulder, then looked at the end of the barrel to be certain it was clear, then looked at Caleb and said, "I'm good, it's okay. Bet I get one before you!" she challenged with a smile.

"Won't neither," declared Caleb in a whisper. Looking at Scratch, he signaled their readiness. Scratch signaled Kettle and positioned himself beside a kinnikinnick bush with his left elbow on his knee and ready to shoot. Several minutes passed as they waited almost breathlessly before Scratch signaled them to be ready. The blast from Kettle's rifle startled the two youngsters, but they quickly rallied and squeezed off their shots along with Scratch. Without waiting for the smoke to clear, they quickly reloaded and aimed for another shot. The animals were startled but confused and were milling around giving the shooters another shot. Within seconds the smoke clouds from the four rifles settled across the tall grass and the hunters watched as the herd showed nothing but light colored rumps as they ran away.

The small herd was strung out as they raced to escape the thunderous threat that had downed several of their number, but within a short distance, they were surprised when the six warriors rose from the grass and let fly with the murderous arrows. Several of the large animals stumbled and fell, some even doing a somersault before coming to rest for the last time. The speed of the elk allowed only one shot from the archers and the surviving bulls disappeared over the slight knoll to the North. Cheers rose from the archers as they celebrated their kills and motioned to the shooters of their success.

When Jeremiah heard the shots from the hunters, he motioned to the now resting villagers and the trek was resumed. Waters rode alongside her husband as they reached the Shoshone creek and began to cross. When they cleared the willows, the two searched the valley for the hunters and seeing them waved to them and looked to each other with broad smiles of approval for the success of their youngsters.

The rest of the village was crowding them as the people pushed their way into the valley to see the site of their winter home. Many expressed their joy as they looked at the lush grass and greenery of the wide valley which was such a contrast from the drought stricken and burned mountains they had fled. Seeing the hunters waving to get their attention and to summon the villagers to help with the butchering, many started at a trot to join the successful hunters, while others continued their journey into the valley and the site of their new camp.

Turning to Waters, Jeremiah said, "Let's go see if Shield and Pine Leaf are okay. I'm surprised they aren't down here already." Looking back at the people, she knew they wouldn't need her help and she was glad to join her husband. The location of their previous camp was less than half a mile from the creek and they crossed the grassy valley quickly. Spotting the break in the trees that marked the trail to the camp, Jeremiah reined his steel-dust forward to lead the way for the two of them. He was cautious because of the silence of the timber, and apprehensive as to what he would find. He signaled to Waters to stop and drop to the ground. He loosened his pistol in its holster, motioned for Waters to ready her bow, and slowly walked to the campsite.

At the edge of the clearing, he stopped to survey the camp. It was immediately evident the camp was abandoned. Nothing remained of the supplies, shelter or anything that would say the camp was occupied. Stepping to the fire circle, he felt the ashes. Cold. They both began to scan the camp for any sign and they spotted tracks that appeared to be several days old. Tracks of several warriors and sign that both Shield and Pine Leaf had been taken.

SHIELD WATCHED HIS CAPTORS AS THE PARTY MOVED along the narrow trail that followed the Shoshone creek. His wrists were bound with rawhide, but they were in front of him so he could handle his horse, but his feet were tied together with a long rawhide strip beneath the belly of his mount. If his horse were to stumble or fall for any reason, Shield could not free himself. When he returned to his camp and was taken by the Crow, there were five warriors but now an additional four had joined them.

He could only make out a few of the words as the newcomers excitedly reported their discovery. It was enough for Shield to know his people had made the journey to the winter camp and would soon discover his absence. At Pine Leaf's insistence, Shield had not been mistreated but was bound and guarded closely. Pine Leaf followed the leader of the Crow, Black Buffalo, who Shield thought was her father. There were four warriors between Leaf and Shield and another four that followed him.

He was taken captive late in the day and the group had traveled for two to three hours before they camped the night before. The first stretch of the trail had been easy going and they passed through a narrow but green valley before making camp. Now they were traveling on a narrow trail on the shoulder of a large mountain of the Absaroka range. The trail was wide enough for easy travel but not wide enough for two abreast so the party moved in single file along the flower strewn shoulder. Blue Lupine and bold orange Indian Paintbrush flowers made brilliant splashes among the tiny flowered low growing Phlox. The bright sun splashed across the mountain side and trickled to the valley below and reflected off the fast moving water of the Shoshone creek.

Looking ahead, Shield noticed the ridge of granite that sloped off the towering mountain and ran across the shoulder that held the trail. A break in the granite wall gave evidence of the trail that narrowed and bent around the imposing barrier of granite. Without slowing, the caravan continued.

Once around the granite wall, the valley narrowed into a semblance of a canyon carved by the chuckling stream now a hundred feet below. The trail was nothing more than a shelf that clung to the edge of the canyon wall and as Shield looked past his left moccasin, he could see almost below his feet the thin silver ribbon that was the splashing water fighting its way through the rocks and bouncing white in the many cascades.

The horses carefully picked their way along the

narrow trail but never hesitated as they followed one another. The path appeared to widen about fifty yards ahead and as Shield looked along the trail, suddenly his horse rolled a rock under his hoof and stumbled to his knees and froze. Startled, Shield tried to grab a handhold on the sheer cliff wall on his right side, but his hands just slid along the wet smooth granite.

Shield felt himself sliding along the neck of his horse and leaning back he sought to allay the slide as the toes of his moccasins grazed the ground below. But his tied feet prevented him from being able to dismount the nervous horse and he pushed with his bound hands on the withers and the jumbled mane. The horse began to tremble and Shield reached down and patted him on his neck and spoke softly to him to settle him down, then leaning far back to put his weight over the horse's rump, taking a deep breath and steadying himself as much as his tethered feet would allow, he tugged on the braided reins to signal his mount to rise. With the horse using the strength from the taut rein and shifting his weight to his hind feet, he stretched one leg in front of him, then pushed up to bring his other leg under him.

Standing still, he trembled and for the moment refused to move. Then when the shaking lessened, the horse turned his head to look at Shield with a soft eye that said, "We made it." Shield realized he had been holding his breath and now let it out and sucked in lungs full of the clear mountain air, looking down at the stream below he realized he could very easily have been nothing but scattered bones and flesh decorating the protruding rocks on the face of the cliff below him. The warriors that followed now jeered and taunted him to keep moving. Shield gave leg pressure to the ribs of his mount and the two moved forward to close the gap with those at the front of the caravan.

As the trail continued along the Shoshone creek, the canyon gave way to an open valley that provided an easier trail that continued to the northeast with the tall peaks of the Absaroka range now peering over the right shoulder of Shield. As the long shadows of dusk stretched across the creek and valley, the trail they followed turned back to the east and began to ascend the shoulder of a finger ridge that extended out from the Absaroka. With the thick black timber swallowing the trail, the party of Crow found a likely camp site for the night and Black Buffalo signaled to his men to prepare the camp.

Two of the men approached Shield and one reached underneath the belly of his mount and untied the rawhide binding his feet together. No sooner had the binding freed his feet and he was roughly drug to the ground with his hands still tied and he was unable to brace his fall. With his face in the dust, the men kicked him and grunted their disgust, but reached for his bindings and pulled him to his feet.

Tying another length of rawhide to his bindings, they pulled him to a large ponderosa, threw the end of the rawhide over a stout branch well above Shield's head, then both men pulled the strip of rawhide and lifted Shield to his toes and pushed him against the tree trunk. While one tied off the strip that held him suspended, the other quickly wrapped another piece around the trunk and the waist of Shield and pulled him tight against the rough bark with dripping sap. Both men grunted their satisfaction and turned to join the others near the now blossoming fire with strips of red meat suspended on green willow boughs.

As the tight binding cut into his wrists, Shield's hands began to numb and he felt the numbness moving down his arms. Without circulation, he would soon lose any feeling in his arms and then pain would begin and would soon be excruciating. But he could show no weakness or fear as he wondered what his fate would be with these the sworn enemies of his people. He knew that the usual treatment of a captive would be severe beatings and mutilation and death and that would usually happen within moments of capture.

If he was younger, he might be used as a slave, but a proven warrior could not be trusted as a slave and would prove more trouble than he was worth. Pine Leaf had implored her father for his life, but there had been no indication that Black Buffalo cared to show any heed to his daughter's supplications. Shield's stomach growled as the aroma of the broiling meat drifted to his nostrils. His last meal had been the day before when he and Pine Leaf had their noon meal and the trials of the day had sapped his strength. Pushing himself up as far as his toes would allow, he relieved the tension on his wrists, if but for a few moments. He knew he was facing a painful night and his mind began to churn.

What will they do? Am I facing torture and death? But those latecomers said my people had made it to the winter camp, maybe White Wolf will come. These rawhide bindings are too tight to twist out of and when they tie my feet . . . it can't be too much further to their village, then what? Will Pine Leaf do anything? She seemed to be afraid to return to her village and I thought of having her join our village, but that will not be now.

With his face against the sticky bark of the ponderosa and his thoughts chasing each other through his mind, he did not hear the approaching footsteps. Pine Leaf spoke softly, "Broken Shield, are you all right?"

"Yeah, just hanging out here with my friendly tree," he replied sarcastically.

She snickered as she moved to his side to see his face and smiled as she reached forward with a knife and cut the strip binding him to the tree, enabling him to move away from the rough and sticky bark. She then reached up and cut the strip that suspended him from the branch and he dropped to his feet and his legs almost gave way as he caught himself and leaned against his most recent best friend, the ponderosa.

In her other hand she held a couple of thick strips of warm broiled meat and extended them to Shield. He readily grabbed the meat with his still bound hands and barely feeling what he gripped, he brought it to his mouth and sunk his teeth into the juicy steaks. Leaf reached for his hands and brought the knife up to cut his bonds. Shield watched as she sawed at the multiple strips of rawhide and he continued to chew while the strips hung from his mouth and bobbed up and down with his chewing motion.

Leaf looked up at him and said, "You look like a hungry dog that will wolf down his meat almost without chewing." She then reached up to wipe off some of the juice as it streamed down his chin to his throat.

Shield looked furtively toward the warriors gathered around the fire and asked Leaf, "What does your father want to do with me?"

"Usually, he would have killed you by now. You are an Arapaho and you were with his only daughter. But I told him you were my captive and he could not because you are mine," she said with a smirk.

"I was your captive?" he asked, unbelieving. "You were almost dead and I took you to my camp and took care of you. It is only because of me that you still live!" he declared vehemently.

She smiled at him and ducked her head a bit as she looked at the ground and said, "I also told my father I want you."

Shield looked at her and reached out and put his finger under her chin gently and lifted her face so he could look into her eyes. "What do you mean, you want me?" he asked softly.

"I want you . . . to live . . . and to be . . . " the statement started softly but then with a boldness that only a proven leader and warrior could show, she looked him straight in the eye and finished with, ". . . my mate."

He looked at her without moving, then lowering his hand from her chin he let a smile begin to tug at the corners of his mouth and he slipped his arms around her waist and pulled her to him and held her close as they spoke softly in each other's ears of their future. At the fireside, they were watched by her father, Black Buffalo and a broad shouldered warrior that sat beside him. He-

who-walks-with-wolves had long sought to have Pine
Leaf as his mate but she was a pipe bearer and war leader
and he had not gained that stature within his village but
he was determined that she would be his or no-one's. He
had a tall broad roach that covered his head with the rest
of his hair hanging loosely to the sides and back. His
broad shoulders and chest showed the scars of the Sun
Dance and from other conflicts in battle. He stood and
stretched as much to show his bulk in a threatening
manner as to take the measure of the bond now evident
between Leaf and Shield. "Waaugh! That is not right. He
is an enemy of the people! She is a war leader and should
not have a mate that is not of the people!"

"It is not for you to say! You have no claim and you
are not part of the council!" exclaimed Black Buffalo.

Walks With Wolves leaned back and roared at the
tree tops. "Waaaugh! I will show you who is worthy!" He
angrily stomped away toward the horses and freeing his
mount from the tether, he swung aboard and kicked his
mount to disappear into the black timber. Black Buffalo
rose and walked toward Leaf and Shield. "My daughter
tells me you fought against the Blackfeet and you saved
her life. This is so?"

"Yes," replied Shield.

"She say she wants you as a mate. She is a war leader
and pipe bearer of my people. Are you worthy of her?"

"I too am a leader among my people. My father was
the leader of my village, but he died in the recent fire and
now our leader is Black Kettle, my uncle and our
Shaman. But he tells me I will soon be the leader."

Black Kettle looked long at Shield and noted his scars

and strength. "When you fought the Blackfeet, did you fight well?"

"There are many that walk with their ancestors now," replied Shield. Although many would brag about their accomplishments especially those in battle, Shield was not one that thought it necessary to measure his worth or deeds.

"Do you want her as your mate?" asked Black Buffalo with the concern of a father as well as the leader of his people.

"Our blood already runs together as we tended each other's wounds from the battle. When I found her and she was barely alive, I knew I wanted her but I did not know her. Now, I'm not so sure, she seems to be pretty hard to control," he answered with a smirk, knowing her father understood, "but maybe with time . . ."

Leaf looked at Shield as her mouth dropped open and then at her father and quickly realized the two men had found common ground in their mutual love for her, but she interrupted with, "What makes you think I'm ever gonna let you control me? I am a war leader and I am the one that controls!"

Shield looked at Black Buffalo with a question in his eyes. Buffalo motioned to Shield to join him by the fire and said, "Come with me, I will tell you how to control these mean women." The two men walked off leaving Pine Leaf standing with her hands on her hips as she watched the two men in her life depart together to conspire against her, and she was happy.

It was a joyful and excited group of Arapaho
that scattered across the valley floor to help in the work of
skinning and butchering the many elk that had been
taken by the hunters just moments before. This was
usually women's work but the hunters and other warriors
joined in this harvest of fresh meat. It had been some
time since the many villagers had an occasion to be happy
in and this was a good sign for their move to the winter
camp.

With the drought and fire in the Wind River Range
that had limited the numbers of game animals and the
harvest of the usual wild plants and vegetables, this first
take of meat for their winter stores was encouraging and
an indication of better days. Each elk carcass was
surrounded by several chattering women and children all
excitedly trying to do their bit to help and to get their
share of the fresh meat. There would be a big celebration
this night and much of the meat would be consumed, but

a lot would be smoked and preserved for the coming winter.

Into this melee walked White Wolf and Laughing Waters with somber faces. Trailed by the big black dog, Two Bits, the couple searched for Black Kettle to tell him about the disappearance of Broken Shield. Their expressions betrayed the message when Black Kettle observed their approach. "Shield?" was the simple question that told of his insight.

"Yes, he is gone from the camp and there was sign that many others were there and took him. I believe it was the Crow that came for Pine Leaf," stated Jeremiah.

"If there were none that lived, how could they know?"

"There were two or three that ran away, whether Crow or Blackfoot, I don't know. But even if no Crow lived, they would come looking for the missing war party."

Nodding his head, Black Kettle knew Jeremiah was right and he lifted his eyes to survey the valley and the tree-line of the towering Absaroka Mountain range. With a wave of his arm he asked, "Which trail did they take and when did they leave?"

"We didn't follow the sign but came here to tell you. But looking at the direction they took from the camp, I think there's a trail that follows the creek through that cut yonder between those two peaks. It was probably three or four days ago, I reckon. I figger to take out after 'em come first light," stated Jeremiah solemnly.

"You will need others to go with you, if they let him live they will take him to their village and there will be too many warriors."

Jeremiah had been thinking about the possibility that Shield could already be dead. Seldom were proven warriors taken captive and allowed to live for any purpose other than the sport of torture and humiliation. His concern was that he would find the mutilated body of his friend somewhere on the trail. He also considered what he might be able to do to free Shield if they found him still captive. Taking a prisoner from a village of your enemy would be challenging at the least and possibly suicidal at the worst.

"Well, I'll take Scratch for sure, maybe He Who Talks to the Wind, and I'm not sure about any others. Maybe Badger and Raven, but no more than that, I'm thinkin'," surmised Jeremiah. "I'm not aimin' to start no war or nuthin', just get Shield back. If I take too many, we'll be easily seen and considered a major threat. It might be possible to just go in and mebbe work out a trade or sumpin'."

"I will speak to Black Badger and Raven Walking. They will be ready before first light," stated Black Kettle as he turned to continue preparations for their winter camp. Most would make a simple camp for this night and the setting up of lodges and making the many brush huts for those without other lodges would take place on the morrow. This night would be for the celebration of the fresh kill and the new home for the village. Yet the celebration would be tempered with the awareness of one of their number being held by the hated Crow.

Waters had left her husband with Black Kettle and went in search of Caleb and Clancy Mae for their help in preparing their camp for the night. She found the two by the big boulder they used for their shooting platform and engaged in a playful debate as to which one dropped the first elk and if Clancy had dropped the second one she claimed or if Caleb's shot had brought it down. They stopped the argument when Waters approached. Her expression warned them of something that would affect their activities for the evening.

Two Bits raced past Waters to greet his friend, Clancy Mae, and jumped up putting his massive paws on her shoulders and dwarfing the girl, now evident only by the red hair that contrasted with the thick black fur of the dog. She rubbed him behind the ears with both hands and spoke briefly to him before pushing him down to see what was troubling Waters.

With hand motions and brief comments, Caleb was dispatched to secure a cut of fresh meat and Clancy joined Waters to prepare their camp. Waters led the way into the timber to the previous camp site occupied by Broken Shield and Pine Leaf. The horses and mules were tethered to the nearby trees and awaited the removal of the heavy packs and the single travois. Both women set to work with the only conversation being the instructions concerning the packs and other gear. Before they finished unpacking the animals, they were joined by Jeremiah and Caleb. When Caleb dropped the elk quarter to the large rock by the fire circle, he blurted out, "All right, who's gonna tell us what's goin' on? Somethin' ain't right and I wanna know what it is!"

Before he finished his question, Scratch joined the family and squatted down near the fire circle and began to rub the big dog behind his ears, yet looked askance to

Jeremiah. Both Waters and Jeremiah stopped and looked at the youngster that had spoken so belligerently then Jeremiah began, "Shield has been taken captive by the Crow. He and Pine Leaf were to wait for us here and the only sign shows a group of warriors took him and headed off thataway," nodding his head in the direction of the narrow trail through the nearby pines.

"Oh, so what're we gonna do 'bout it? We're goin' after 'em ain't we?" asked Caleb.

"We're leavin' at first light."

Clancy quickly asked, "All of us?"

Jeremiah smiled and shook his head as he said, "No, you will stay here and help Waters prepare our camp and help with the many others that still need to be tended to for healing." He looked at Waters and noted a slight narrowing of her eyes and firmness to her expression. She took a deep breath and returned to the task of unpacking the animals. Jeremiah motioned to both Scratch and Caleb to help with the packs and taking the animals to the small grassy meadow to be tethered.

Clancy went to Waters side and spoke softly to her, "We could do just as good as they can, maybe better. 'Sides, you're better with a bow than any 'o them three and I can shoot as good as Caleb." Listening to the girl express some of her own thoughts made Waters aware of the hard decision made by her husband. She knew he would rather have her by his side than any other warrior, but she also knew he was very concerned about her pregnancy and didn't want her exposed to any danger that could hurt her or the baby.

Her own thoughts about going after the Crow and

her life-long friend Broken Shield were much the same as Clancy's but she also knew that her husband's decision was right. With a heavy sigh, she turned to her new daughter and said, "Yes, but the people need us. And if they," motioning toward her husband, "are not successful, they will need us to go and rescue them," she said with a mischievous smile spreading across her face.

While Clancy attended the meal preparations, Jeremiah provided the muscle to help Waters erect their teepee. The lodge was the one they used during the first months of their married life before Jeremiah built the log cabin in the clearing where Jeremiah and Ezekiel had their first cabin. The first three lodge poles were tied together near the small end of the poles, then pulled erect to form the base tripod.

The additional lodge poles were laid into the cradle formed by the first three with the base of the many other poles forming a large circle. The lodge covering was of buffalo hide and provided a weather tight covering over conical stacked lodge poles. The lodge covering was pulled up one side and then spread out around the circular frame with the opening facing to the East to catch the first rays of the morning sun. There would be ample room within the teepee for the entire and now extended family to have sleeping space as the base of the teepee measured about sixteen feet across. With the lodge erected, everyone made busy to put much of the gear and personal items within the lodge and to spread out their sleeping robes around the perimeter. The very center of the circle was reserved for a small fire for warmth and in inclement weather, for cooking.

After the filling evening meal of fresh elk steak, baked yarrow root with wild onions, and corn bread, the tired family chose to turn in for an all too brief night's rest. Caleb thought he had just fallen asleep when Scratch nudged him with his foot and whispered, "C'mon squirt. We gotta get a move on." Rolling out of his robes, Caleb pulled on his moccasins and stretched out for his powder horn, possibles pouch, and knife and scabbard. He joined the two men outside as Scratch led their horses into the camp to be saddled and packed for their journey.

They had just completed their gearing up when Badger and Raven rode through the trees to join the trio beside their horses. Slipping their rifles into the scabbards, Jeremiah, Scratch and Caleb mounted up and with a nod and a wave to Waters and Clancy as they stood by the lodge, the party rode through the dark trees into the grey light of the slow approaching morning.

THE CLEAR BLUE SKY OF THE EARLY HOUR AND THE brilliance of the morning sun revealed the beauty of the narrow valley of green that wiggled its way between the towering granite mountains as it followed the cascading creek on its way to the distant valley and lake far below. They were on an easy trail that followed the creek into the small valley. The tracks left by the party of Crow, although occasionally obscured where the wind had blown the dry sandy soil, were easy to follow for the Crow had done nothing to hide their sign.

Jeremiah led the way followed closely by Caleb on his strawberry roan, then Badger and Raven with Scratch bringing up the rear. The five moved as silently as possible with the only sounds made by the hooves of the horses occasionally clattering along the sometimes rocky trail.

As was his habit, almost unconsciously, Caleb would mimic any animal sounds he heard as they traveled. First there was the chatter of a squirrel that busied himself gathering his winter store of nuts that stopped in mid-stride on the branch of the pine and looked at the intruders to his domain. With another chattering reprimand, he started to his lair, but was stopped by the answering chatter from Caleb.

They continued on their way and shortly were greeted by a sizable hawk that circled overhead and let loose his screeching warning from above, only to be answered with the echoing call from below. It was easy to see the hawk turn his head mid-flight to examine the source of the answer. Scratch was watching Badger and Raven as they turned and searched for the source of the sounds with confusion written on their faces. He chuckled remembering the time Jeremiah and Caleb had tricked him before he knew of Caleb's ability to mimic the sounds of any animal with precision and clarity that could fool even a seasoned mountain man like himself.

As the path broke from the trees by the edge of the canyon and the impending shelf trail, the whistling challenge of a bull elk was plainly heard not too far away. When Caleb cupped his hands to his mouth and answered the challenge, Badger realized the source of the sounds was the young man known as He Who Talks with the Wind. He turned and motioned to Raven and signaled him to look at Caleb as the youngster again answered the challenge of the distant bull elk. The brothers smiled and nodded their heads in understanding and chuckled to themselves at this new revelation. The tension that wore heavily upon each of them from the beginning of the day now flitted away with the echo of the bugling call to the bull elk.

All of the mounts had been proven on the trail many times before, but when the five horses started along the shelf that hung from the side of the cliff, there was a nervousness with the horses that bore Badger and Raven. Fear can be contagious especially among animals and the stutter step of the bay gelding ridden by Badger was repeated by the paint mare ridden by Raven. Both horses leaned into the cliff wall and kept their eyes on the trail in front of them.

Scratch could see the tenseness in the backs of the two warriors that also refused to look to the canyon below them. It appeared that neither horse nor rider breathed until they reached the end of the shelf trail and approached the smooth path on the shoulder of the mountainside. Scratch muttered a "Thank you, Lord," and breathed a little easier as he followed the brothers that now were considerably more relaxed. *It's kinda funny how the two o' them could go from laughin' at Caleb's elk bugle and then be so scairt at a little bitty narrow trail. Oh well, mebbe they'll be better when we git to them trees yonder,* thought Scratch.

The long day was dropping the curtain of darkness when the small band of travelers determined to make camp. Shortly after entering the black timber, the campsite previously used by the Crow was chosen by Jeremiah for their camp. As the men tended to their horses, removing tack, brushing them down, and tethering them near the water and grass, Jeremiah scouted the campsite. As he examined the sign from the previous occupants, he spotted the strip of rawhide hanging from the tree branch at the upper end of the camp. Looking at the tracks below, he was confused by the tracks and the marks on the tree that indicated a captive, probably Shield, had been bound there.

It looks like they tied him here, but if he was here all night or for a long period of time, the bark on the tree would be worn off more and there would be more tracks or something, but it looks like he was just here for a little while. Maybe they let him down and bound him for the night, or what? I'm not sure.

Jeremiah motioned for Scratch to check out the sign and see what he thought. "From what I can tell, he was shore tied up here, but for how long or what they did, I don't know. But at least he was still alive when he was here," motioned Scratch as he looked back at Jeremiah.

"Yeah, that's about all I can figger out too. We'll just have to see what the rest of the trail tells us tomorrow."

"I'm all for that. I'm so hungry, my belly button's pinchin' my backbone! What say we get some vittles and some shut-eye. We kin hit the trail before first light and see what we kin find then."

Jeremiah nodded his agreement and the five men stretched out on their bedrolls for a cold camp of jerky, pemmican and water before rolling up in the robes for a well-deserved rest. First light would come all too soon.

The searching rays of sunrise peeked through the thick timber to find the five well on their way. With the eastern sky painted a brilliant orange, the color was reflected on the green pines giving the trees an odd color devoid of shadows. The morning light was suffi-cient to reveal the tracks of the party of Crow that marked the trail before them. There was nothing to indicate they moved with any haste nor had there been any attempt to obscure the trail and Jeremiah believed the party of Crow was not fearful of anyone following them.

*Could it be they just believed their village could easily repel any attack and they were not concerned if anyone followed them to the village? Surely not, no village would want to be attacked. Or could it be . . . nah . . . but what if . . .if Shield went with them willingly, they wouldn't think about anyone attacking them or trying to free him. Nah, that can't be . . .*thought Jeremiah.

Scratch had been watching Jeremiah trying to work out some problem by talking with himself and making arguments by waving his arms. He had seen his friend do this many times before, it was his way of working out any problems or making plans and Scratch always got a chuckle out of the many facial expressions he saw on his friends face.

"So, who's winnin' the argument?" asked Scratch.

"What?" said Jeremiah as he turned to see the smile stretching across the face of his friend, "oh, I was tryin' to figger out the puzzle of the tracks. They don't seem to be too concerned about somebody followin' 'em."

"Well, could be they are tryin' to lure us into a trap. Ya think about that?"

"Actually, no, I was thinkin' more about them not bein' afraid of anybody followin' and I also thought it might be cuz Shield coulda gone with 'em willingly."

"It seems to me, the only way we'll know is if we just keep on'a goin' where we're goin'. Just keep a good eye out for some kinda ambush, and if they don't jump us purty soon, mebbe we'll just have'ta sneak up on 'em after they get to thar village."

"Yeah, I reckon you're right," said Jeremiah somewhat dejectedly as he turned to watch the trail before him. The mountain trail wound through the thick timber toward a saddle that broke the line of a long finger ridge before them. Judging by the lay of the land, Jeremiah believed the other side of the ridge would reveal the valley on the Eastern side of the Absaroka Mountain range.

Some years before, Shield, Waters and Jeremiah had taken an extended hunting trip that brought them up the valley of the Greybull river and Jeremiah believed this trail would take them near the headwaters of that same river. As he brought up the memory of that trip, he knew that location would be in the heart of Crow country and would be a good site for a winter camp for the Crow village. There was plenty of water, grass and the wide valley was nestled between a pair of tall finger ridges that would provide protection from fierce winter winds.

The switch-back trail continued to climb toward the crest of the ridge before them as the timber thinned out with a scattering of fir and spruce. Several pockets of Aspen gave a contrast of colors and Jeremiah noted that some were beginning to turn colors to the rich gold of the fall. It would be several weeks yet before the aspen and oak began to strut the colors that would paint the hillsides, but when the aspen in the high country began to lose the green and the quaking leaves started to show hints of yellow, the cooler days of fall were not far away.

Thinking of the change of seasons, Jeremiah's mind

brought thoughts of Waters and the new winter camp. He wanted to build another cabin before the new baby arrived and the snow settled in, but they might not have time to complete a build. But they had spent more than one winter in the snug buffalo hide teepee and they could again. The clatter of hooves on the rocks brought his attention back to the trail.

As the last switch-back of the trail brought them nearer the crest of the ridge, they were in the open with the only cover from the windy pines. These were trees that yielded to the strong winds of the higher elevation and held limbs that grew only on the downwind side with the upwind bark showing red from the frigid breezes. Usually stunted in growth, the windy pine seldom reached a height of more than seven or eight feet and provided little cover for the travelers. Jeremiah raised a hand to stop the procession before they crested the ridge and sky-lined themselves. He ground tied the steel dust gelding and walked hunched over to the ridge to look into the valley on the other side. In the far distance, about four or five miles, he saw a wispy cloud of smoke that revealed the village of the Crow.

DUSK CAST LONG SHADOWS ACROSS THE TRAIL THAT dropped at an angle over the face of the long ridge that stretched across the head of the valley. Shield sighted the village nestled in the edge of the trees in the upper reaches of the widening valley that held the headwaters of the Greybull River. Black Buffalo led the party of Crow warriors into the village to the greetings of all that witnessed the entry. Shield scanned the village and the inquiring faces of the many women and children.

It was easy to see the expectancy was mixed as some had hoped for the return of their missing men and others joyful at the return of the war leader Pine Leaf and a few somewhat perplexed by the Arapaho that rode beside Pine Leaf. As Shield continued his survey of the village he noted the many teepees of buffalo hide, several painted with scenes of deeds or emblems of the family that lived there. Beside one was a woman sitting in front of a frame that held the hide of an elk she busily scraped while her infant watched from the nearby cradle board.

To the edge of the camp there were several children playing a hoop game where one would roll a hoop ring while others would cast their "spears" in an attempt to pierce the ring. The children were oblivious to the returning party and continued their play and shouting without interruption. Some of the women tended cook fires and the meal preparation for the evening meal while others were seated in circles and busied themselves with making moccasins or other articles of clothing from deer or antelope hides. Shield noted little difference between this village and the one that had been his home as he grew to adulthood.

Black Buffalo stopped in front of a large lodge and slipped from his mount. Pine leaf also dropped to the ground and motioned for Shield to join her. A boy of about ten summers quickly took their horses to turn them out with the village herd. The horse herd was below the camp in the wider stretch of the green valley and was the largest herd for one village that Shield had seen.

Numbering well over two hundred, there were enough horses for every warrior to have four or five mounts and many for carrying lodges and other needs. The Crow people were known for raising fine horses and for being shrewd horse traders and horse thieves. Most of the raiding parties were more for stealing horses than inflicting death or even counting coup on an enemy as the horses were the greater prize to these people.

As they turned toward the lodge, Shield looked around and noticed a tripod of poles to the side of the entrance that supported an elaborately painted and decorated shield with scalps and feathers dangling in the breeze. Attached to the shield was a long lance that was similarly decorated and Shield knew this was the lodge of the chief or principle war leader and the shield and lance signified his many accomplishments and honors earned in battle. He was a respected and even revered leader but Shield's brief acquaintance with the man had shown him to be wise in the way of his people and a very knowledgeable leader.

His dignified stance he now assumed before his lodge was expected of him upon his return from a successful though somber journey and he now waited for his wife to exit the lodge to greet him on his return. The entrance flap was flipped aside as a mature and matronly woman stepped through the entry and rose to stand beside her husband, but her eyes settled on Pine Leaf and she lost her composure and immediately ran to her daughter with arms spread wide. Buffalo looked at her with chagrin and glanced at Shield as both men watched the reunion of the women. What dignity the chief had was gone as he dropped his arms to his side and motioned Shield to follow him into the lodge. As the chief bent to enter, Shield could hear him grumbling something about "women!" in a very negative tone.

Shield was able to communicate with Black Buffalo with the same mixture of Crow, Arapaho and sign language that he used when talking with Pine Leaf. Buffalo was a little more fluent in the Arapaho language than Leaf and Shield found it easier to carry on a conversation with the man.

"'That woman is supposed to greet her chief before she does anything, but you think I can get her to do that? Not when her daughter has returned! She better have food prepared or I might have to teach her a thing or two when I put her over my knees," complained Buffalo. "Her daughter is just like her. Are you sure you want her for a mate? You might regret it when she gets old and fat and sassy like her mother," he said smiling.

Shield knew the older man was just grumbling because that's what a returning chief was supposed to do or at least that's what they always did anyway. But Shield returned the smile and simply nodded his understanding to this man that he had already grown to like and respect.

Buffalo continued, "We had given up on Leaf ever finding a mate. When she became pipe bearer, the men respected her but most were afraid of her because she was a better warrior than any of them. The only one that wanted to be with her, He Who Walks with Wolves, she didn't want to have anything to do with him. She wouldn't even take him on any raids with her!" He seated himself before the fire ring and motioned for Shield to also be seated. He went on, "What did you do that made her think you would be a good mate?"

"Well, my brother, White Wolf, and I fought the Blackfeet and I think she saw me on the hill above the battle. But after the battle she was unconscious and we took her back to our camp and she tried to kill me there, but when she saw I was only tending her wounds she started looking at me a little different. We both were thinking the same thing but neither of us said anything about it, we just talked about everything else. I think we both knew almost right at first but you came along before we could really talk about it," he said with the last of his comment coming with a bit of a disgruntled tone that wasn't missed by Buffalo.

"Don't you know that's what fathers are supposed to do?" he chuckled. "She told me some about the battle and your tending her, but not much about the battle. What happened?"

Shield related the details of the Blackfoot ambush and the ongoing battle, expressing regret they were not able to do more to save more of the Crow. When asked as to why they intervened, Shield explained the Blackfeet were his enemies as well, and he couldn't stand by and watch them massacre others- even the Crow.

Buffalo listened intently and nodded his head in understanding as his guest continued to detail the battle. Shield explained about his expectancy for the Arapaho to have their winter camp in the valley on the other side of the mountains and why they had to leave the Wind River Mountains and their usual winter camp. Buffalo watched this younger man and thought that he truly would be a good mate for his daughter and the union could bring at least a truce between the villages if not the two peoples. With the number of warriors in his village diminished by the recent fight with the Blackfeet, it would be good to have the assurance of peace with this village of Arapaho.

The lodge flap was flipped aside and the bent figure of Black Buffalo's woman entered and quickly stood before Shield and looked at him with a stare that could strip the fur off a cat-tail at twenty paces. After several moments of glaring down at the intruder, she motioned in the direction of Pine Leaf and said, "You will go to her lodge, but she will stay here. There is much to do before you are coupled tomorrow after the noon meal." Then turning away without even a change of expression, she began preparing the meal for her husband and with her back turned to Shield, he was dismissed.

Pine Leaf motioned for him to follow her as she exited the lodge. As he stepped out to join her, she took his hand to lead him to her dwelling. As a war leader, she had her own lodge even though it was not usual for a woman without a mate to have her own. She was proud of the teepee and entered the darkness to quickly light a fire in the ring in the center of her home. Using a flint and steel, she soon bent to blow on the embers at the bottom of the prepared stack of kindling and wood and brought the embers to a dancing flame that blossomed into a fire that lit the entire shelter.

Standing to her feet, she watched Broken Shield as he looked about and noted her many possessions and trophies of battle displayed throughout. She had earned many honors and taken many trophies including scalps and weapons from the vanquished. These were visible around the interior and it was also evident this was occupied by only one person and that was a woman, even though she was a proven warrior. Turning to Leaf he said, "I didn't know we would be joined so soon. Your mother said it would be tomorrow after the noon meal?"

Leaf looked at him questioningly, "I thought you would be glad, but you are not?"

He smiled back at her, "Yes, I'm glad. Just surprised, that's all."

She nodded happily and clasped his face between her hands and said, "I'm glad too. Just looking at you makes me happy and soon we will be one." She then turned and left him alone in the lodge and he thought, *But what about a meal? I'm hungry!*

As Jeremiah turned away from the crest of the ridge, he noticed Scratch kneeling beside his horse in the trail and looking at the tracks and sign at the edge of the path. He reached down and crumbled a horse dropping in his hands and looking up at the returning Jeremiah said, "You know, we be only a day, mebbe less, behind 'em, don't ya'?"

"Yeah, when we started out I was thinkin' we were most of two days behind 'em, but I been noticin' the sign too. That's good, maybe they ain't had time to do whatever it is they got on their mind," commented Jeremiah as he turned to the other three that traveled with him. "Here's what I'm thinkin' 'n Scratch you jump in any time you think. Let's back off this ridge a bit and make camp down there in the trees, an' 'bout first light we'll work our way through those trees on the other side and around the uphill side of their village. Maybe even split up, but we'll see 'bout that when we get closer. We'll watch what's goin' on for a while before we decide our next move. We

be way outnumbered, so we're gonna hafta be real careful. But for right now, let's back off down there aways an'
make us a comfortable camp for tonight."

Scratch nodded his head and led his mount past the
three younger members of the party to head into the
timber and a likely campsite. He had noticed a likely spot
as they started up the trail and like any seasoned mountain man, catalogued it for future use. He just didn't think
the future was going to come upon him so soon. As they
worked their way back to the camp, Jeremiah followed
the four as his mind recalled the image of the village and
the surrounding terrain. He was concerned about his
friend, Broken Shield, but he also had to be mindful of
the safety of these that traveled with him. He was totally
confident in Scratch and even Caleb, but Raven and
Badger were still unproven as far as he was concerned.

They had earned the right to be chosen warriors for
this and other endeavors, but riding with a large party of
warriors out to do mischief and riding with mountain
men was two entirely different things yet Jeremiah knew
these sons of his mentor, Ezekiel, had much of their
father in them. Although the big black man known as
Buffalo Thunder had died when the boys were still very
young, their mother and uncles had trained them well.

Camp was soon made and horses tethered well away
from the trail and all agreed it was too close to the village
to risk a fire. Another cold camp meant their meal was
once again buffalo jerky and pemmican with fresh water
from the snow melt fed stream nearby. White Wolf
encouraged them all to turn in early as they would have
to be on the trail before first light in the morning. No

argument was given and within a short time the differing sounds of slumber mixed with the many sounds of the night

. The narrow stream nearby came from a small glacier near the top of the ridge and fresh water always attracted a variety of life in the mountains as it chuckled down the mountainside. The rustle of early fallen quakie leaves told of some small four-legged creature of the night searching for a meal, perhaps a chipmunk or even a bobcat. The middle of the night heard the hoo-hoo, hoo-hoo of a great horned owl as he asked his question of the darkness.

Caleb spent a restless night of wonder at what the morrow would bring and how he would do on this mission of rescue. He also listened closely to the night sounds as was his habit for no sound escaped his attentive ears and mind. He knew some of the Native tribes thought the cry of an owl was a sign of death or trouble, but he thought of it as nothing more than another call to learn and mimic. Nearer the dawn, Caleb listened as a red-tailed hawk started his early hunt as he circled high above and used his high-pitched, keeeeer cry to startle his game into movement. While the owl was a sign of trouble, the hawk was a sign of good fortune and the conflicting sign just verified Caleb's belief that those beliefs were best left to the Indians.

Jeremiah, or White Wolf, nudged his son with the toe of his moccasin to let him know it was time to rise and ready himself and his mount for the task of the day. All the others turned-to as Jeremiah woke each one in turn and within moments, the five were trudging up the trail and trusting their mounts to see what they could not as they again bit off chunks of jerky to let it soften in their mouths and provide the mornings nourishment.

Formed by the hand of the Creator and carved by the many storm run-offs, the finger ridges extending north eastward from the Absaroka Mountain range simulated the fingers of a large hand with differing lengths and shapes. Separated by sometime deep ravines, the smaller cross ridges formed by runoff that bled from the ridge hugging snow caps now allowed cover for Jeremiah and company. He had chosen an observation point directly south of the village on a well elevated ridge that held a thick covering of black timber.

Well concealed, Jeremiah and Scratch now looked down on the village that was tucked into the edge of the timber but still open enough to catch the now blazing morning sun. They watched the village come awake with several warriors exiting their dwellings and disappearing into the nearby woods for their morning constitutional, soon to be followed by the women going a different direc-tion. While cook fires were stirred to flames by the women, Jeremiah motioned to Scratch toward several of the warriors that went separately to a small knoll to make prayers before the rising sun.

"They ain't so different from the rest of us are they?" stated Scratch in more of a statement than a question. He thought, *If more people could accept that we ain't all that different, maybe we wouldn't be goin' 'bout killin' each other and just let the other'n live his own life.*

The two men were able to seat themselves and lean back against the large towering ponderosa to continue their observation. The scattered boulders and scrub oak brush just off the top of the ridge provided enough cover yet did not obscure their vision of the valley below. Scratch reached into his possibles bag and brought out a brass tube to show to his friend.

"Take a look-see through this hyar thing. It's one o' them tellyscopes like them ship's captains use out on the ocean."

"How'd you get your hands on this?" inquired Jeremiah.

"Traded it from some pilgrim that had give up on the idée of settlin' out West and needed some wherewithal to get back to the city."

Lifting it to his eyes, he stretched out the tube of the telescope and scanned the village below. As he moved the scope about, he paused as he saw a familiar sight in front of one of the conical dwellings. "Shield," he whispered just loud enough for Scratch to hear.

"He's just standin' there, ain't nobody even payin' him no mind. He ain't a prisoner!" Jeremiah stated with confusion furrowing his forehead. Dropping the scope and turning to Scratch he repeated, "He ain't a prisoner, what the devil is goin' on down there?"

Scratch reached for the telescope so he could view the picture that had upset his friend. The imposing figure of the muscular Arapaho was easily spotted by Scratch. Even though it had been a few years since the last time he saw Shield, he easily recognized the burly warrior. While many of the Crow warriors made a tall roach with their hair and had braids that dropped to their shoulders, Shield always wore his hair straight and loose and longer than shoulder length. Tucked behind his ears, the straight hair hung onto his chest and down his back and added to the regal look of the proud warrior. He spoke with no one but stood comfortably with his arms to his side as he watched the activity of the Crow people before him. He appeared to be waiting for someone although no one appeared to be watching him.

"Yep, yore right about that boy. Ain't nobody payin' him no mind at all. He shore 'nuff ain't no prisoner as far as I can tell." Then dropping the scope, he looked at Jeremiah and said, "That shore puts a different spin on things now don't it? Whatcha thinkin' we gonna do?"

"I don't know. Guess we'll just have to wait it out a spell and see if we can tell what's goin' on. He may not be a prisoner, but if we go waltzin' in there uninvited, we'd sure end up all trussed up like a Christmas turkey, I'd bet."

————

Black Buffalo strolled toward the lodge of his daughter in search of Broken Shield. Seeing him standing before the dwelling, he greeted him with "*Kahee*" the usual greeting of the Crow. Shield nodded his head and smiled as Buffalo motioned for him to seat himself before the entry of the teepee. He was joined by Buffalo as the two men sat cross-legged and faced the warmth of the morning sun. "This is a big day for you, my son," stated the older man awaiting an acknowledgement.

"Yes, Uncle, it is," answered Shield, using the term of respect toward the elder.

"I talked with Pine Leaf about the bride price," said Black Buffalo looking at Shield. The younger man turned to the elder, swallowed and ducked his head as his thoughts ran rampant. The tradition of most tribes was for the suitor to bargain with the father of the bride to arrive at a mutually acceptable price. It wasn't so much as buying a bride as it was the opposite of the old tradition among the whites of providing a dowry that accompanied the bride.

In the manner of the Indian, the bride price was to replace the value of the daughter as she left the family. Within most of the plains Indian tribes, theirs was a matriarchal society wherein the ownership of things such as the lodge and other property was held by the woman and the genealogy was also traced through the woman. If a mating didn't work and the woman wanted to end it, she would simply place the personal belongings of the warrior outside the lodge and he would not be allowed to return. With such value placed on the side of the woman it was only right that her value be replaced to the parents.

"I had thought she would bring many horses and perhaps other trade goods," stated Black Buffalo with a somber expression on his face, "but she tells me you saved her life and brought her back from the great beyond when you took care of her so my woman says that satisfies the need for a bride price," he concluded smiling. The mischievous side of the respected elder and leader of the village once again showed itself to Shield.

"She is indeed worth a great bride price and I have thought of that," he said rising to return to the dwelling of Pine Leaf. When he returned, he held out what most would consider a gift of much greater value than several horses. Contained within a scabbard of soft tanned deerskin decorated with beadwork and quillwork designs, rested his treasured Hawken rifle.

As he extended the treasure with one hand, the other held the necessary powder horns and possibles bag with bullet mold and lead. Black Buffalo rose to his feet and his eyes brightened and a smile spread across his normally somber face as he held out his hands to receive the gift. He would be the only member of the village to have such a treasured weapon and he practically glowed at the thought as he cradled the beautiful rifle in his hands. Shield was pleased with Buffalo's acceptance of the bride price and knew this man would proudly display what all the others within the village would covet.

Lowering himself to be seated again, Buffalo motioned for Shield to join him. The elder began to explain what the events of the day would be and what would be expected of him. The two men sat facing one another and the animated conversation was viewed but not heard by two men sitting on a distant hill and watching through a brass telescope.

BROKEN SHIELD LIFTED HIS EYES TO THE CLEAR BLUE sky that arched over the village without a cloud to be seen. The early afternoon sun splashed the valley with brilliance that warmed everyone that stood waiting for the ceremony to begin. Standing next to Black Buffalo, Shield looked toward the Crow leader for some indication of the event to start but he stood stoically and unmoving. Two lines of women standing shoulder to shoulder stretched from Pine Leaf's dwelling to the center of the large clearing where the men waited.

Suddenly, the women began a cacophony of noise. Some held hand drums and beat them rhythmically with small sticks, others beat sticks together, and still others had conical shaped metal resembling bells that they beat upon with mallets. The noise became a steady rhythm accompanied by the keening and singing of the many women as they looked to the entry of the lodge in anticipation of the appearance of the bride. At the edge of the clearing, a large drum centered in a circle of older men all with large padded drum sticks, sounded forth with the steady beat that could be felt by those nearby.

This was a grand celebration and not just a normal joining of two people. This was the daughter of their chief and one of the favored war leaders to be joined to a sub-chief of another people. The people were happy and their exuberance carried through the entire celebration. The rhythm and singing rose to greater volume as the flap of the teepee was thrown back and the moccasin of Pine Leaf touched the ground. When she exited and stood her mother stepped from the dwelling behind her and stretched to place the headdress of feathers upon her head. All the noise makers froze as they looked at her and there was just a moment of complete silence. She was a bride, but she was also a warrior and pipe bearer and war leader and it was only fitting she wear the full ceremonial headdress of her people. Once it was placed upon her head, the rhythm of the drums began again but this time the singing was stilled to a simple hum of the women's voices.

Shield sucked in a deep breath as he sighted her down the long gauntlet of women. A white doeskin dress draped her body with splashes of color and fringe. Around the neck of the dress was a wide band of blue and white beadwork outlined by a double row of elks' teeth in a scooped half circle that accented her slender neck. Across the yoke above her breasts was another row of blue and white beadwork interspersed with intricate designs with porcupine quills.

Down the length of the arms was a row of small conical tin bells that shone silver in the bright light.

Around her waist was a wide beaded belt with blue and white designs in the shape of diamonds within diamonds and the ends of the belt trailed down her left hip. The skirt of the dress had three more parallel rows of matching beadwork also with intermittent designs of porcupine quills. The long fringe of the sleeves and on the bottom of the skirt each had a piece of fringe end with a puff of white rabbit fur and a bright blue tassel of dyed buckskin. She wore tall moccasins of soft white doeskin bearing elaborate beadwork across the toes and up the sides that matched the dress.

Two braids hung from under the headdress and each braid was interwoven with white ermine fur. A broad bone choker necklace with turquoise was wrapped around her neck. Every move she made as she walked the gauntlet was accented with the splashes of color and the tinkling of the silver bells, but what caught Shield's attention more than any other was the broad smile showing white teeth and pure joy and the sparkle in her eyes as she approached him.

When she joined him, they locked arms and turned together to face White Beaver, the shaman of the village. He was adorned with a white fur headdress with buffalo horns mounted on either side and wearing a long tunic of buffalo hide that was painted with many different designs signifying his prominent position as the Holy Man of the Crow People. Almost unnoticed was the tunic and leggings worn by Shield that matched the dress of his bride.

Medicine Bird had insisted he wear them and she was not one to argue with since she was soon to be his mother-in-law. The actual ceremony was short and Shield did not understand all that was said, but he nodded his head when he was supposed to and listened attentively as if he did. The shaking of a gourd rattle over their heads signified the end of the vows and everyone shouted and the drums began again.

———

Watching the activity in the village, Jeremiah stood mesmerized holding the spyglass and seeing his friend standing in the middle of the entire Crow village and arrayed in typical attire for some celebration. Handing the telescope to Scratch he said, "Just what in the world's goin' on down there, see if you can figger it out."

As the sourdough lifted the brass tube to his eye he asked, "Whatcha think's goin' on?"

"Unless I miss my guess, he's gettin' married," he stated somberly.

"Married?!" asked Scratch as he lowered the telescope to look at Jeremiah.

"Well, look see. But I think I'm right about this."

While Scratch watched through the scope, Pine Leaf walked toward the waiting Shield and when the two locked arms to turn to the Shaman, Scratch said, "Well, I'll be hornswaggled. By Jove, I think you're right." He handed the scope back to Jeremiah so he could see the ceremony.

Jeremiah stood transfixed as he witnessed the joining from afar knowing his friend would be thinking about the presence of his parents and friends. When the ceremony ended and the people shouted and started dancing, Jeremiah had a thought. Summoning Caleb to his side, he said, "Son, we got a job to do, you and me." Then he turned to Scratch and explained what he planned and asked him to keep Badger and Raven with him while they carried out his plan.

Caleb followed Jeremiah closely as they worked their way silently through the timber and down the hillside toward the village. Stopping near the edge of the trees, Jeremiah instructed Caleb on his task and the boy slipped away to move farther around the village still staying in the trees. Talks to the Wind found a likely spot in a small copse of trees not too far from the nearest lodge. He lifted his hands to his mouth and faced away from the lodges and began the high piercing cry of the Hawk with a *Keeeeeer* and as he stretched the cry out he slowly turned to face the village. Then again with another *Keeeeeer* that faded away to the other side. He quickly stepped back into the thicker timber and started back to his father's side.

Upon hearing the cry of the hawk, several looked up trying to spot the circling hawk but without sighting the bird, continued with their dancing. Again the cry came and Shield looked heavenward and when no hawk could be seen, he thought about Talks to the Wind. He looked around for some indication of his friends but seeing none, he turned back to his bride. A short while later, he again heard the cry coming from the other side of the village and he immediately knew it was Caleb. Smiling broadly, he looked at Pine Leaf and said "My friends have joined us. They are nearby." She gave him a puzzled look and thought about the cry of the hawk and realized that it was Shield's friends that made the sound. She said, "Your friend is very good. I have never heard anyone make that cry so perfectly."

"And he is only a boy," stated Shield smiling broadly, "they will wait for us on the trail. You will see them tomorrow." He turned to look to the hillside with the dark timber and smiling broadly he put his right arm across his chest to his left shoulder and with his hand flattened, he extended his arm straight out in front of him then dropped it to his side. This was a sign that "It is good," used by most people versed in the common sign language. He knew his friends would see this and would meet him tomorrow. If he did not come, they would return to the village without him.

Jeremiah and Caleb returned to their observation point where Scratch and the others waited. As soon as they appeared, Scratch said, "He signed that he knew you were there and that he was okay. I figger we'll wait for him on the trail and maybe meet up with him tomorrow. Is that what'chur thinkin' too?"

"Yeah, either they'll come with us or he'll at least come out to talk to us and then we'll know what our next step's gonna be. So, let's head back to that same place where we camped last night and we'll wait for him to show up. Ya reckon?" asked Jeremiah.

As Scratch walked down the back side of the ridge to the waiting Badger and Raven, Jeremiah and Caleb followed behind. With less concern about being seen, the five returned to the camp along the same trail that they traveled just a few hours before. But this time they would have ample daylight left so they could have a cook fire and a good meal for the night. Different thoughts filled the minds of each of the travelers as their horses moved along the dusty trail and mounted the ridge that promised fine fixin's and a night's rest, hopefully.

HE WAS SEATED ON A GREY LOG AT THE EDGE OF THE little creek that cascaded down the hillside seeking the larger stream that was the beginning of the Greybull River. Jeremiah enjoyed the chuckling of the water that splashed about the rounded stones and bounced white from one to the other. It was a soothing sound and one that befitted his time in prayer. He watched as the searching golden rays sought a passageway through the towering pines to cast their glow on the sprigs of life that struggled through the pine needles beneath the tall trees.

Looking at the blue and white columbine flowering alongside the stream he was reminded of the colors of Pine Leaf's dress and his thoughts were dragged back to the present. Returning to the camp, he noted that all were stirring around the small fire and waiting for the brewing coffee and the sizzling meat strips that promised a good start to the day. After a quick meal, Jeremiah asked Caleb to walk up to the trail and keep watch for Shield.

"Stay out of sight, we don't know if he'll come or if someone else from the village might come up the trail. If it's Shield and Leaf and no one else, let us know, give a Marmot chirp but if it's anyone else, a hawk." With a nod, Caleb grabbed his Hawken and started uphill through the trees toward the trail. Because of the tracks left by the group, it was important to know who would be coming because their sign would easily be seen and they would be found. The last thing Jeremiah wanted was to have some conflict that could ruin the good that came from the joining of Shield and Pine Leaf.

The sun was no more than a hands breadth above the horizon when the two mounted riders were silhouetted on the rim as the trail crested the ridge. Caleb recognized Shield on his paint gelding and was assured the second rider would be Pine Leaf. She sat astride a solid built buckskin with the signature black mane, tail and long stockings that marked the buckskin color. She sat tall and proud and was no more than two strides behind Shield. Caleb could hear their voices as they seemed to be chattering like a couple of chipmunks.

Turning downhill, Caleb called out with the typical chirp of the high mountain dwelling marmot. Repeating the chirp, he started downhill through the timber to rejoin his father and the others. Shield and Leaf would follow the switch-back trail to make their way down the steep mountainside. There were three switchbacks to the trail before it leveled out on the shoulder of the mountain to make its way into the lower valley. The last twist to the trail was within about fifteen feet of the edge of the sheer drop off to the stream that cascaded over a hundred feet below. The camp where Jeremiah waited was near the second sharp bend in the trail and set back securely in the timber. Caleb quickly made his way straight down the hillside to the camp to tell Jeremiah of the soon arrival of Shield and Leaf.

The newlyweds were happily chattering and laughing about the last few days and the many possibilities of the future. They had already agreed their first home would be with the Arapaho. When a war leader is defeated or loses her warriors in battle, that leader would not easily be followed again and would often lose the honor in shame. However, because of her standing and previous honors, she was still considered a pipe bearer and war leader, but by joining with Shield she believed the most honorable path to take would be join with her husband as he assumed what would be his new role as the leader of his people. They were eagerly anticipating the response of his people when they arrived at the winter camp and their discussion was about their new home and the hopes of starting a family. Those pleasant thoughts and the happy talk was suddenly interrupted when a screaming figure launched from a roadside boulder with and ear piercing *Aaiiiieeeeee* and slammed into Shield taking him to the ground.

The five would-be rescuers were packed and mounted as Jeremiah held the lead on the strawberry roan for Caleb. The boy quickly mounted and the group started back to the trail to await their friend. As Jeremiah neared the trail he turned to look uphill anticipating the appearance of his friend and his bride, suddenly he was startled by a shrill scream and a shout. He spurred his horse up the trail in time to see two men scrambling to their feet on the downhill side of the trail. He recognized Shield and could immediately tell the other was intent on shedding the blood of his friend.

Shield had started to turn to look at his bride behind him when he saw the movement from the boulder above him. Looking up he saw the man flying through the air with an upraised war club and Shield braced himself by hunching down and grapping the mane of his mount. The force of the impact tore him from his horse and the two men were sprawled on the down-hill side of the trail.

Rolling over into a crouch with his hands and feet firmly on the ground, Shield looked at He-Who-Walks-With-Wolves snarling like a rabid wolf and grabbing at his waist for his knife. Wolves had lost his war club in the fall but wasted no time searching for it but grasped his knife and rose to a crouch with the weapon extended before him. Shield also rose to a crouch and reached to his belt and withdrew his knife.

Baring his teeth in a snarl, Walks-With-Wolves said, "Now I will show you who is worthy of that woman. You will see how a Crow warrior can cut out your heart and eat it. I will feed your carcass to the animals if they will have you." The slope of the hillside hindered the usual action of knife fighters of circling one another. Both men sought the uphill side, knowing an assault from uphill would be hard to defend.

Pine Leaf shouted, "We are already joined. You cannot change that and I wouldn't have you anyway!" She spat at him to show her distaste and hatred for the betrayer of her people. What he was doing would be enough to get him banished, not just from the village, but from any Crow people.

"When he is dead, you will see who is a real warrior!" Wolves shouted over his shoulder, refusing to take his eyes off Shield. This man looked too calm, too relaxed. *He should be afraid, I am Walks With Wolves! He is nothing but an Arapaho, they are like buffalo dung!*

Shield wasn't afraid, but he was wary and he was confident. He had never been bested in a knife fight but he knew this fight was to the death and he could not be careless. He slowly moved his knife back and forth a short way, never too far, just enough to keep Wolves attention. Holding it with the blade up, he made a slight feint forward and quickly withdrew.

Moving his feet just enough to feel out the ground and his footing, he kept swaying his body. With a quick lunge, Wolves dove toward Shield expecting to drive his knife into his belly, but a sudden last second twist of his torso, the blade went past throwing Wolves off balance and Shield brought his knife in a sweeping motion across the attacker's back, drawing blood.

Wolves quickly spun around to again face Shield, now Shield had a slight advantage with his knife arm on the uphill side and he knew Wolves would expect him to attack with a lunge with the weapon. Instead he made a slight feint to catch his eye then Shield brought a round-house swing and slugged his big fist into the side of Wolves head knocking him to the ground. But the Crow pushed himself up and brought his knife around in another sweep reaching for Shield. The sudden move caught Shield slightly off balance but he sucked in his gut and arched his back away as the blade slit his tunic and nicked his midriff and drew a fine line of blood. Seeing the red on his knife, Wolves grinned and slathered with a guttural growl and said, "Now you die, you Arapaho scum."

Again he lunged at Shield who quickly sidestepped but as the Crow's arm was outstretched Shield clamped down on his wrist with his left hand. Dropping his knife from his right hand and bringing his hands together to encircle the wrist of the Crow, he forced the arm up before the face of Wolves and said, "This is what we do with those who betray their people."

He stretched the arm upwards and with a sudden downward force, he snapped the bones in Wolves arm with a crack that echoed across the canyon. The scream from the man resembled the scream of a woman giving birth and Wolves, now on his knees and holding his arm searched the ground for his knife. He stretched his left arm for the knife and Shield backhanded him, knocking him to a tumble and without a good arm to catch his balance, he tumbled over and over down the steep hillside, through the scattered timber, and with nothing to stop his descent, he disappeared over the rim of the canyon. His scream of terror echoed through the canyon until he was silenced upon the rocks below.

Jeremiah and the others stood frozen and silent. Pine Leaf also was still and quiet as she sat on her mount looking down at her man with pride. Shield turned to the men waiting on the trail standing by their horses. "Are you going to lead your horses or ride them?" he said smiling at his friends. "We have a long way to go and you will get tired if you don't ride them."

"We was gittin' a little saddle sore chasin' you all over the country so we thought we'd just stretch our legs a mite," replied Jeremiah soberly. "But if you're done runnin' I guess we oughta just mount up and go home."

SITTING ASTRIDE THEIR MOUNTS AT THE EDGE OF THE trees as the small cut in the mountains made by the Shoshone creek opened to the wide green valley the two men looked at one another and again at the expanse before them. Shield spoke softly to his friend, "You have been true to your word."

"Ummm Hummmm," replied Jeremiah, "we did as we said, didn't we? I think this will be a good camp for this winter, especially after the sacrifice you made."

Shield looked questioningly at his friend, and Jeremiah explained. "You know, goin' and gettin' married so there'd be peace between the people 'n all." His sober expression soon spread into a broad smile. Pine Leaf nudged her horse between the friends and said, "For a long time I hated all white people and fought them. But Shield convinced me they were not all bad. But if you keep it up, I will change my mind again," she warned with a grin. Then turning to Shield, she said, "Take me to meet your people, or are you waiting because you are afraid?"

The people had been busy and much had been accomplished in the few days Jeremiah and company had been absent. Those with hide lodges had erected them in a semblance of order with most set back within the trees and the tops of the many teepees could be seen peeking out of the pines. Others had lodges of both hides and brush that were in the rounded top style similar to the wickiup of the southern tribes. But the village was busy with all manner of activity from the curing of elk hides and the smoking of meat to the playing of children. The return of the men raised a raucous shout and the villagers gathered to greet the returnees. Most happily greeted them but it was evident that many showed concern and questioned who was this woman with Shield? Stopping before the lodge of Black Kettle, Shield dropped to the ground and motioned for Leaf to join him. Black Kettle exited his dwelling and stood before his nephew with his arms folded across his chest and awaited the proper introduction.

"Uncle, this is Barcheeampe or Pine Leaf, pipe bearer and war leader of the Eelalapito Crow people and my wife," and turning to Leaf, "This is Black Kettle, our Shaman and leader of our people."

It was usual for a woman to bow her head when introduced to a leader or elder of the people, but as a war leader or woman chief, Pine Leaf held her head high and spoke, "I am honored to meet the leader of the people. My husband and I ask the right to live among the people and be one with you."

Black Kettle smiled and said, "I am honored and happy to see my nephew has found an equal as his mate. We will be pleased to have you as one of The People."

A loud shout erupted as the entire village cheered and crowded around to meet the mate of the man who would soon be their leader. This would call for celebration and feasting and the women soon dispersed to begin the preparation for this occasion. Waters stood next to her husband and her arm rested around his waist as she looked up at her man and said, "This is a day I never thought we would see. He has always been so picky! I'm happy for him and I think she will be good for him."

"Like you've been good for me?" asked Jeremiah.

"Well, at least this time, you didn't bring home another son or another daughter," she said as she watched Caleb and Clancy talking together at the edge of the crowd.

"I think you've already taken care of that," said Jeremiah as he patted her protruding belly. "We're gonna have to get that cabin up pretty quick before you pop!" he kidded and put his arm around her shoulders.

"Oh, I don't know. Our lodge is pretty cozy and it will do fine if we need it to, and I'm not sure you'll have time to get a cabin built before this one joins the family," she said smiling.

Like most husbands, what Waters said seemed to go right through his head without his ever catching the meaning of her mischievous hint of things to come.

The celebratory feast was enjoyed by all and served as a special christening of their new home as well. It was an optimistic crowd that ate, danced and sang well into the early hours of darkness that night, but soon the drums fell silent to be replaced by the many sounds of slumber of a safe and happy people. Jeremiah lay with his hands behind his head as he thought of the many events that brought him to this point in his life.

Faces of the past flitted through his memory, his Mother and Father and sister, Ezekiel, his mentor and adopted father, Ezekiel's Momma Sarah, the freed slave woman, the many friends on the wagon train that were lost to the tornado, Shield's family lost in the fire and others. But the thoughts of those with him in the lodge, his family, were the ones that filled his heart with joy. He never thought he would be a father and husband and friend to so many. His was a rich life and he was happy. He rolled over in his robes and was soon fast asleep.

Well before dawn, Jeremiah stirred awake and missed Waters. *Maybe she's just making one of her many trips to the woods like she's had to do so often lately,* he thought. But something nagged at him, so he rose and slipped on his moccasins and grabbing his pistol, he slipped from the lodge to find his wife. Walking quietly into the woods behind their lodge, he found nothing. He turned to make his way among the other lodges still searching but moving quietly. Nearing the uppermost edge of the village, a large hide covered brush hut had light from a fire escaping the edges of the doorway hide covering.

He could hear voices inside and recognized the voice of his wife. He reached toward the opening to scratch the side to seek entrance when a sudden squall and groan startled him. He froze where he stood, then heard a small cry come from within and he realized what was happening as the joyful chatter of women confirmed his thoughts. Another robust cry from a little one announced the birth of Johnathan Jeremiah Ezekiel Thompsett and Jeremiah shouted loud enough to wake the entire camp. His proud smile provided enough light for anyone nearby to know what the shout was about.

THE END

The making of a man is a challenging metamorphosis by any standard, but when it's in the wilderness and among the Arapaho people, the standards are raised. Such was the challenge of Caleb, the adopted son of Jeremiah Thompsett and Laughing Waters. With his Pa a proven warrior and leader for the people and his Ma becoming the new Shaman for the village, Caleb naturally wonders about his future and the possibility of marrying his sweetheart and spending their lives living in the wilderness with his people, the Northern Arapaho. With confusion and frustration confounding his thinking, he follows the council of the elder of the people and his Grandfather, Black Kettle, and departs for the Bighorns and a vision quest to the sacred Medicine Wheel. Seeking the many answers to the questions that have plagued him, he looks to his God for direction for his life, his manhood, and his companion.

Returning to his home with what he believes to be the needed direction and the answers he sought, he is confronted with tragic news of the kidnapping of the love of his life. Questioning himself and his purpose again, he is joined by his Pa, Jeremiah, and their partner, Scratch, as this odd collection of mountain men, young and old, sets off in pursuit of the renegade kidnappers and the needed retribution. With obstacles before him and a fight awaiting him, he must push through his trial by fire to find his beloved.

AVAILABLE NOW FROM B.N. RUNDELL AND WOLFPACK PUBLISHING

Born and raised in Colorado into a family of ranchers and cowboys, B.N. is the youngest of seven sons. Juggling bull riding, skiing, and high school, graduation was a launching pad for a hitch in the Army Paratroopers. After the army, he finished his college education in Springfield, MO, and together with his wife and growing family, entered the ministry as a Baptist preacher.

Together, B.N. and Dawn raised four girls that are now married and have made them proud grandparents. With many years as a successful pastor and educator, he retired from the ministry and followed in the footsteps of his entrepreneurial father and started a successful insurance agency, which is now in the hands of his trusted nephew. He has also been a successful audiobook narrator and has recorded many books for several award-winning authors. Now finally realizing his life-long dream, B.N. has turned his efforts to writing a variety of books, from children's picture books and young adult adventure books, to the historical fiction and western genres which are his first love.

Printed in September 2023
by Rotomail Italia S.p.A., Vignate (MI) - Italy